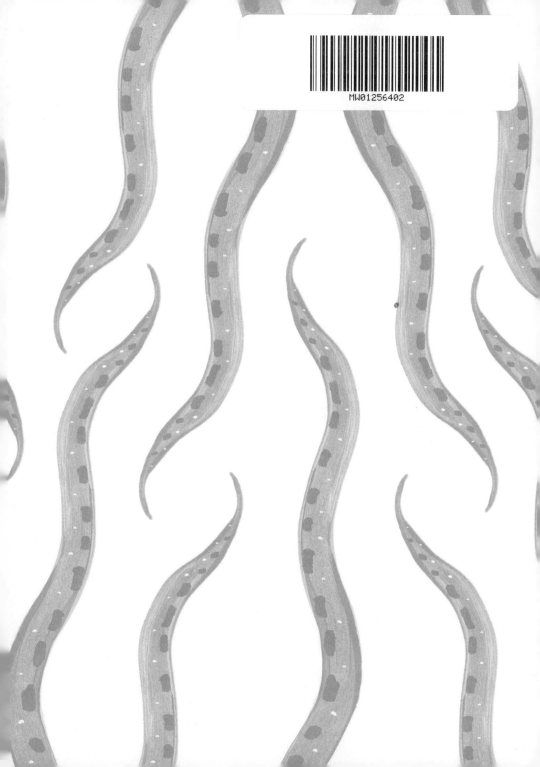

# My Presentation Today is About the Anaconda

This is an Em Querido book

Published by Levine Querido

LEVINE QUERIDO

www.levinequerido.com · info@levinequerido.com

Levine Querido is distributed by Chronicle Books, LLC

Text copyright © 2022 by Bibi Dumon Tak

Illustrations copyright © 2022 by Annemarie van Haeringen

Translation copyright © 2025 by Nancy Forest-Flier

Originally published in the Netherlands by Querido NL

Library of Congress Control Number: 2024941096

ISBN 9781646145102

Printed and bound in China

Published in February 2025

First Printing

The publisher gratefully acknowledges the support of
the Dutch Foundation for Literature.

**N** ederlands
   **letterenfonds**
dutch foundation
for literature

# My Presentation Today is About the Anaconda

### by Bibi Dumon Tak

#### Illustrated by
#### Annemarie van Haeringen

#### Translated by
#### Nancy Forest-Flier

LEVINE QUERIDO

Montclair | Amsterdam | Hoboken

# TO START OFF...

These are oral presentations given by animals about other animals. That's because oral presentations can really be fun, especially when they're not being given by the human species for once. After all, humans can make presentations super boring.

Why?
Because humans only look at things through their own human eyes.
Every single time.

Human after human.
Kid after kid.
Class after class.

YAWN!

So it's time to take a fresh look:

Animal after animal.

Here we go!

# 1

"HELLO,
I'M A CLEANER FISH,
AND MY PRESENTATION
TODAY IS ABOUT
THE SHARK.

"Sharks have a reputation for being serious bad guys. They eat fish and octopuses like there was no tomorrow. To us cleaner fish they look like torpedoes, the way they chase their prey through the water. It makes us chuckle to see how the other fish panic when a shark shows up. Sometimes sharks even hunt in groups so they can close in on their victims. One big gulp and that's it, because the mouth of a shark is huge. Escaping is impossible. Once you're inside a shark's mouth you'll never live to tell the tale. Except if you're a cleaner fish like me. Today's presentation isn't about cleaner fish, though, but about sharks.

"Cleaner fish run their own cleaning service right from home. By home we mean the coral reef. Any fish that feels grubby can stop in at our cleaning station. And some fish can be really gross. I often wonder if they hadn't put it off a little too long. Their fins are crawling with parasites—those tiny critters that live on the skin and scales of water animals. Some of our customers carry half a zoo on their bodies.

"We serve everyone, no questions asked. We scrub fish of all shapes and sizes, let's put it that way. But this presentation isn't about fish in general, it's about sharks in particular. That's because sharks are my favorite customers, which is why I've decided to talk about them.

"The shark is my favorite fish because he has those yummy leftovers between his teeth. And boy, does he have a lot of teeth. More than you can count. They're white and pointy. The lower teeth are smaller than the upper ones, and everything gets stuck between them. That's what we scrub away. If we didn't do that, the leftovers in the shark's mouth would cause an infection. We cleaner fish keep the shark's teeth in tip-top condition.

"After taking care of the shark's teeth the cleaner fish check the rest of the body for wounds. Sharks have plenty of wounds because of the wild life they lead. We really like the pus in the wounds and the bits of dead skin. Sometimes a whole team of cleaner fish gets in on the act because sharks are humongous—they seem a mile long to us. Most of the yucky stuff is concentrated around the gills and fins. We remove all that junk as part of our treatment. *All-inclusive*—that's the professional term we use. But anyway, I was going to talk about sharks today, not about cleaner fish.

"While we cleaner fish are working on a shark we can just relax and take our time. It's a disgusting job, but we love what we do. Sometimes the sharks forget to keep floating while we're cleaning them

and they sink to the bottom like dead jellyfish. That's how much the sharks enjoy our treatment, and that's why they don't eat us.

"If a shark wants us to give him a cleaning, he gets super polite. With us, that is. He swims up to our cleaning station and just hangs there without moving a muscle. Sometimes the waiting line can be five sharks long, five good-natured guys who are suddenly the picture of patience. That's how they let us cleaner fish know there's work to be done. As a matter of fact, sharks totally depend on us. Without cleaner fish, they'd die. That's why my presentation today is about sharks.

"There are false cleaner fish out there, too, by the way. I'm serious. They pretend to be ordinary cleaner fish, but when the shark relaxes and spread his fins in the water and starts to sink a little, the false cleaner fish take a bite out of the shark's healthy skin and swim away. Just imagine. The shark is lying on the ocean floor, super relaxed, and looking forward to the gentle lips of the cleaner fish—we cleaner fish are part of the Labridae family, known for their thick lips—and suddenly he gets bit on the butt. Before the shark knows what hit him, the faker fish is gone. That's why these imposters are called false cleaner fish. They don't belong to our honest family of fish, known as wrasses, but to the family of combtooth blennies. Well, if that's the name of the family you come from, what do you expect?

"Now you know everything there is to know about sharks. Oh, yes: sometimes a cleaner fish is eaten by a shark, accidentally or on purpose. It's an occupational hazard.

"Okay. That was my presentation on sharks. Any questions?"

"Yes!"

"What do you want to know, fox?"

"Well, how many teeth does a shark have?"

"That depends on the species of shark, so it's hard to say. It might be a hundred, but it might also be a thousand. A shark's teeth are constantly being replaced throughout his lifetime. As soon as a tooth is worn out, a new one pops in. Let me put it this way: we cleaner fish will always have work. Whether the sharks are young or old, they'll never have cavities."

"Thanks, cleaner fish."

"You're welcome, fox. Any more questions? No? Then thanks for listening."

2

"HELLO,
I'M A BLACKBIRD,
AND MY PRESENTATION
TODAY IS ON THE
ROSE-RINGED PARAKEET.

"The rose-ringed parakeet is a rather striking bird. He's bright green and he has a big red beak, but when he opens it, out comes the most awful sound you ever heard. It's deafening. More deafening than all the traffic in the city, including the sirens some cars have. Not to mention the screaming of children. We blackbirds love the city and the gardens and the playgrounds, but as soon as a bunch of those green tooters come flying in, we're out of there.

"There never used to be rose-ringed parakeets around here. The only place you ever saw them was in cages. But one day their owners let them loose, probably because the owners had gone crazy from all that screeching in the house. The parakeets flew away and had baby parakeets and even more baby parakeets, and now they're all screeching bloody murder in our parks.

"They screech because they're not song-birds. They screech because they can't do anything else. They have no syrinx in their throats, which is the organ that enables birds to sing. Even crows and magpies have syrinxes, and the sound they make is hard to bear. Imagine what would happen if you didn't have any syrinx at all. You'd make the sound the rose-ringed parakeet makes. It would be like a fire alarm going off all day long.

"What they say to each other is a mystery to us blackbirds. It sounds like the rose-ringed parakeet is in a constant state of panic. Or war. His squawking drowns out everything else. If we song-birds were to try to imitate their sound, we'd never sing again, because our vocal cords would be torn to shreds.

"When rose-ringed parakeets aren't screeching, they're destroying things. They snap the buds off the trees, and sometimes they all get together and attack the feeding table in the garden where humans leave food for the birds. They have very strong beaks, so they boss everybody around. They're real hooligans.

"Even so, sometimes I wish I were a rose-ringed parakeet. I bet it's lots of fun, making all that noise. Just letting yourself go—I bet that's fun, too. Blackbirds never let themselves go. Blackbirds live very controlled lives. Occasionally we sing our hearts out, but that's only in the spring, and only the males do that. I'm a female, and sometimes I'd rather be green instead of brown, with a red beak and no boundaries. If I'm honest, some days I'd like to screech until the trees curl. That's why my

presentation is on rose-ringed parakeets: because I secretly admire them.

"Questions, anybody? No? Then thank you all for listening."

3

"I'M A ROSE-RINGED
PARAKEET
AND THAT'S WHY
MY PRESENTATION IS ON
SONGBIRDS.

"Like the blackbird said, I'm not a songbird.

"I can sing—sort of—but according to the other birds my singing is atrocious. They call it screeching.

"Songbirds can really sing because they have this thing in their throats. It's called a syrinx. You pronounce it 'see-rinks.' The syrinx is a vocal organ. I read that on Wikipedia, and the blackbird has already mentioned it. It makes music like a church organ, but you play it with your throat, not with your fingers.

"Get it? Ha-ha-ha!

"So songbirds have a vocal organ in their throats, and that's why they can warble. Wikipedia says that songbirds have special muscles in their throats that cause certain membranes to vibrate.

"I had to look up the word 'membrane' because I didn't know what it meant. Wikipedia says that a membrane is a thin tissue between two spaces. I think the Wiki guys mean that a membrane is sort of like those thin skins you see on the top of a fresh jar of bird peanut butter. So that tissue is a membrane. But it's so small that it fits into a bird's throat. Not in the throat of a swan or an ostrich, because they aren't songbirds, but in the teeny tiny throat of a nightingale, for example.

"Is everybody still with me?

"So these songbirds all have these membranes in their throats like the skins in peanut butter jars. And when the membranes start vibrating, they call it warbling.

"Well, I'd rather eat a whole jar of peanut butter down to the bottom than have it in my throat. But I must say that some birds are really amazing singers. That's why my presentation is on songbirds.

"Of all the songbirds, my favorite is the wren. That's because he's what you might call a super tiny little whippersnapper. I mean, super super tiny. But he makes an ear-popping sound. It's as if he had a mega-membrane in his gullet. Like a ginormous peanut butter jar with a skin as big as sails on a sailboat. Wrens sing super loud. Not only in the spring, but in the winter, too.

"They once organized a contest. By 'they' I mean humans. (I got this information from the internet, too.) They came up with the top hundred most beautiful bird songs. All the birds were allowed to enter the contest, even the non-songbirds. That was really cool, that no bird was left out. As long as you had feathers. We rose-ringed parakeets did our very best, but we didn't make the list. Not even in hundredth place.

"My presentation isn't supposed to be longer than five minutes, so I can't read out all the songbird winners. I'll just tell you the top five, real quick:

blackbird
nightingale
song thrush
robin
wren

"I sort of agree with the top hundred, but not entirely. The wren should have ended up in first place, of course. And what I really don't understand is how the whip-poor-will and the cuckoo made it. Those birds are just saying their own names for crying out loud. At that rate I could win, too, although rose-ringed parakeet is quite a mouthful.

"The whinchat is the big loser of the contest. He ends up at the very bottom, in hundredth place. If you're in hundredth place, you're probably better off not being on the list at all, like us.

"I also wonder what the tawny owl is doing in seventh place. Tawny owls shriek like banshees. Really. We rose-ringed parakeets wouldn't live any-where near them. I mean, there you are, perched on a branch and having a nice snooze, and suddenly one of those spooks comes whizzing by? And in the middle of the night, no less.

"Is my time up? But I haven't finished yet. I'll just scream the rest from the top of the fence."

From the top of the fence:

"The raven is up here, too. In seventy-third place. All he says is 'caw.' Ridiculous.

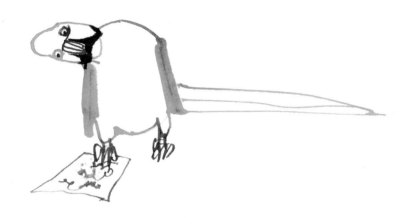

"And the Savi's warbler. That's a small brown bird that zooms around like a motorbike. You never see them, but you sure do hear them. What a racket!

"And what's the buzzard doing in twenty-ninth place? The buzzard is a flying cat! You're thinking: watch out, the four-legged bogeyman is on the prowl, and then this predatory bird comes howling over your head. Twenty-ninth place? Stop it!

"And the sparrow! Seriously, all the sparrow ever says is 'chirp' and that's it. And he's in twenty-seventh place. I repeat: twenty-seventh place. Even the common redpoll sings better than that, right? But the common redpoll is almost at the bottom, like the hawfinch.

"The chiffchaff is in forty-second place. So incredibly boring. He sings the way he looks. All day long, the same old hacking. And how the graylag goose ended up on the list is a mystery to me: 'honk-honk-honk.' That ought to cheer you up, right?

"Fortunately, the heron—like the rose-ringed parakeet—isn't on the list. Those birds scream even louder than we do. So loud you may never hear or see again.

"I actually enjoy the sound of the woodpecker. Really nice. Sometimes we occupy the holes they make in trees for their nests, so they don't like us very much. But we like them. That rat-a-tat of theirs is wild. Sorry, woodpeckers, for pilfering your little holes.

"We should start a heavy metal band: the herons, the woodpeckers, and us. Now that would raise the roof. The bitterns could work the horns in the background. And the wren could be the lead singer.

"Well, that was my presentation. Unfortunately, there's no time for questions."

# 4

"Hello everyone,
I am a midwife toad
and my presentation
today is on
the koala.

"The koala is a marsupial. Many marsupials carry their newborn young around in a kind of pouch on their bellies. Kangaroos do that too, and so do possums. Since I can't talk about all the marsupials right now, I did eeny-meeny-miny-mo and ended up with the koala. Maybe next time I'll talk about one of the other marsupials. But first the koala.

"There are many differences between koalas and midwife toads, but there are lots of similarities, too. I'll start with the differences. That makes my presentation easier to understand.

"The differences:

1. I myself am an amphibian, an animal that can breathe underwater and out of the water. A koala is a mammal that can only breathe out of the water.

2. A mammal means that the young drink milk from their mother. The word "mammal" comes from the Latin word for breast, where the milk comes from. The most well-known mammal is the human being. Amphibian babies take care of themselves as soon as they crawl out of the egg. They don't drink their mother's milk.

3. A baby koala is called a joey. Midwife toad babies are called tadpoles. Koalas give birth to only one joey at a time, but midwife toads can have sixty tadpoles at once.

4. Koalas eat lots of leaves from the eucalyptus tree. They live all the way on the other side of the world, in Australia, where there are no midwife toads.

5. Koalas can live without water because they get their fluids from the leaves they eat. We midwife toads live on the land, but we can't survive without water.

6. Our skin feels cold and bumpy, while a koala's skin feels soft and warm.

7. A koala makes a growling, grunting sound—like a pig, but really low. A midwife toad has a call like a bird. It doesn't sound at all like croaking. When the male midwife toads start calling together at night, it sounds like the ringing of little bells from a herd of cows in the mountains.

"Koala males and midwife toad males both make noise to attract females. And that's where I get to the similarities. Because it was the similarities that made me want to talk about koalas.

"The similarities:

1. Both marsupials and midwife toads carry their young with them. With the marsupials it's the mothers who do the carrying, and with the midwife

toads it's the fathers. Which seems weird, since they're called mid-*wife* toads.

2. When a koala has a baby, the baby is very, very small. As big as a tadpole, but pink. It hardly amounts to anything. After it's born, the teeny tiny joey crawls up the fur of its mother like a little worm until it gets to the pouch. With its mouth it latches on to the nipple where the milk comes out, and it doesn't let go for a very long time.

3. We midwife toads are a little jealous of that pouch. We don't have pouches, even though our males also carry their young around. These aren't live young, however. They're eggs, and the tadpoles grow inside them.

When the female starts laying her eggs, the male gathers them up. The eggs come out of the same opening as our poop and pee. They're attached to a kind of chain. The male pulls the chain of eggs out of the female using his hind legs and winds the chain around them. After the female lays the eggs, she goes off on her own while the male takes care of the children. He carries them around just like koala mothers do. We're the only species of toad that looks after our eggs. Other toads just leave their eggs in the water and pay no more attention to them.

4. When the tadpoles in the eggs are full-grown, the fathers go back to the water and release the chain of eggs. Their job is done.

"A koala mother carries her baby hidden away in her pouch for six months. When her baby is big enough—when it's no longer bald and blind and the joey looks like a real mini-koala, instead of a little pink worm—it climbs out of the pouch and onto its mother's back. It sits on exactly the same place where the midwife toad fathers carry their eggs. That's why I feel a special connection with the koala.

"I've killed two birds with one stone with this presentation. Now everybody knows something about koalas AND something about midwife toads. Giving this talk was lots of fun. Actually, it was a kind of school lesson. And midwife toads enjoy teaching, of course. Are there any questions? Go ahead, rabbit."

"Well, with us rabbits you never know who your father is. It's all kind of mixed up. With the midwife toad you know exactly who your father is, since the male impregnates his wife while he's pulling the eggs out of her. Then he immediately winds the eggs around his hind legs. He knows for certain that he's the father of his children. But how does that work with koalas?"

"What a good question. Yes, koala mothers also know who the father of their baby is."

"How do they know?"

"Uh . . ."

"Just tell us. When it comes to this sort of thing, nothing is too weird for us rabbits."

"What sort of thing do you mean?"

"Making babies."

"Oh, okay. Well, when a koala female and a koala male mate . . ."

"Mate? You mean have sex?"

"Uh, yes. That's right."

"Go on, midwife toad. I'm all ears. Fortunately, rabbits have very long ears . . . ha!"

"Let me put it this way. After mating, the last bit of semen from the koala male hardens. It turns into a kind of clay."

"Woo-hoo!! Guys, did you hear that? The koalas shut the whole thing down!"

"That hard semen makes sure that, uh . . . that the female can't get pregnant again by another male. But I'd rather leave it at that."

"No, we want more. Boy oh boy, how do koalas come up with this stuff?!"

"Nothing is strange, rabbit. All animals are different, aren't they? Although we midwife toads do have a little bit in common with marsupials. Any more questions? No? Then I'd just as soon stop right here. Until the next time!"

5

"I'M A ZEBRA
AND MY
PRESENTATION TODAY
IS ON
PURE BLACK-AND-WHITE
ANIMALS.

"Only a few animals in the world are black-and-white. And I mean, *exclusively* black-and-white. The stork has black-and-white plumage, but his beak is red. So that doesn't count. There are other animals that might seem black-and-white, but they don't meet my requirements.

"The black-and-white ruffed lemur doesn't make the cut because of his yellow eyes. I've got to be strict here. Black and white. So even the zebra long-winged butterfly—which was named after us— has no place in this presentation because of the tiny little dots on the underside of his wings. They're red!

"Black-and-white is not light gray or dark brown or light yellow. I won't be discussing the osprey, the California kingsnake, or the pied butter-fly bat. Those species can give their own presentations.

"My list of black-and-white animals includes six other species besides myself. Fortunately, they're all mammals. There was one bird that had to be removed from my presentation at the last minute: the Adélie penguin. In the first picture I saw of him he was standing in the snow. But his feet turned out to be pink. So, sadly, the Adélie penguin had to be removed.

"Animals that do meet the requirements are:

the European badger
the orca
the panda
the skunk
the Malayan tapir
the colobus monkey

"The world's seven black-and-white animals do not know each other. That's why I'm giving my

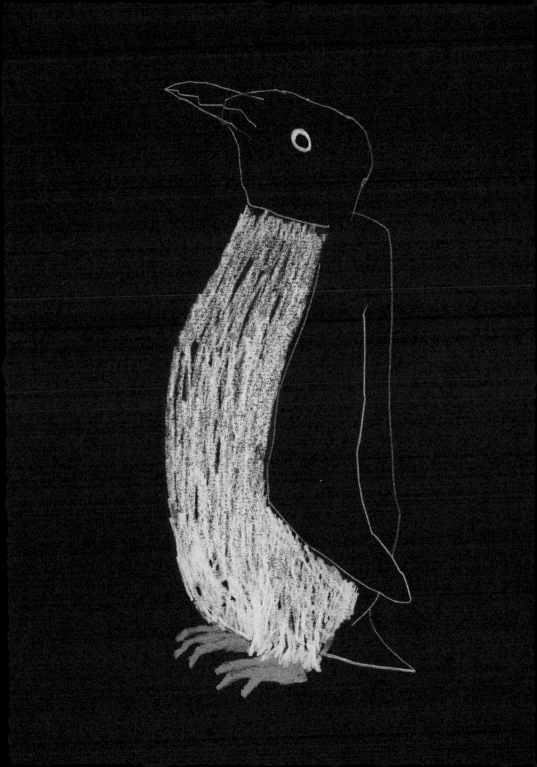

presentation on this small group, because what you don't know is always the most interesting. What you *do* know you already know. You know? I suspect that the other black-and-white animals feel the same way.

"None of us black-and-white animals have ever seen an orca because orcas live in the water.

"None of us black-and-white animals have ever seen a panda because pandas live in China, where there are no other black-and-white animals.

"None of us have ever seen a badger, either. There are Japanese badgers and Asian badgers, but they're yellowish and brownish. Only the European badger is black-and-white. But none of the other black-and-white animals on my list live in Europe.

"Most skunks live in America, and one species lives in Asia.

"The Malayan tapir lives in a very small part of Asia. He may have come face-to-face with a skunk at some point, although there's not much chance of that happening because their habitats barely overlap.

"Finally, the colobus monkey lives in Africa, just like me. Not on the steppes, but in the forests and mountains. From his perch in the trees the colobus monkey may be able to see us zebras in the distance. It's possible. It's not *im*possible. But we can't see the colobus monkey ourselves. He's up there hidden away, and we zebras usually spend our time looking at the ground where the grass is growing, or at the horizon where the lion lurks. In other words, it would be a miracle if one black-and-white animal species were to meet another one in the wild.

"Science still hasn't figured out why some animals have black-and-white fur or skin. Some experts think that if an animal's fur or skin is black-and-white, it makes him appear smaller. Take orcas.

If small fish can see only the white or black parts of the orca, he appears less dangerous.

"In the case of us zebras, the stripes are handy for keeping things like insects away. Black-and-white scares them off.

"All animals know a skunk when they see one. They know that if they mess with a skunk, they'd better not inhale for awhile.

"But it's still not entirely clear. That's why I'm following this subject closely. If there are any new discoveries about exclusively black-and-white animals, I'll let you know. Does anyone have any questions?"

"Yes, me!"

"Let's hear it, ermine."

"How come I'm not on the list?"

"What do you think is the reason, ermine?"

"Well, I am completely white with a black tail, right?"

"Because it's winter."

"So, I don't count?"

"I have to have standards, my friend. In the spring you turn brown again."

"So, can't I count for half the year?"

"Sorry, ermine. You've got hidden color."

"That's not fair!"

"You can't have it both ways. That wouldn't be fair either.

"Anyway, so that was my presentation. If anyone thinks they know of a black-and-white animal that I haven't mentioned, but that meets my strict requirements, they can send an email with photographic proof to equus@quagga.za."

6

"I AM A SNOW LEOPARD
AND MY PRESENTATION
IS ON
THE SNOW LEOPARD.

"I think it's very noble of all the animals in this book to give their presentations on other animals, and I'd like to do that, too, but I must say I am forced to talk about myself. The reason is: no one ever notices us. We're invisible—it's as if we didn't exist. If I hadn't decided to give my presentation on snow leopards, we'd never get any attention. We are a hidden treasure that no one seems to know about. *The snow leopard, who's he? We didn't even know such a thing existed!* You hear the other animals say this all the time. Yet we're a species that some humans devote their whole lives to. The spend all their time on us—I'm serious. And if they ever find us—which rarely happens—they want to keep finding us over and over again, even if it takes the rest of their lives. These humans spend weeks lying in tents in the freezing cold in the hope of catching a glimpse of us, at an elevation of ten thousand feet or more. They wait and wait somewhere between the ice and the void. They drink frozen water. Their fingers and toes freeze off. Their noses turn black, they get lost, go snow-blind, become discouraged and desperate. They count the stars in the night sky to keep from losing track of time. Every time something moves on the other side of the valley, they jump to their feet, because they think they've finally caught sight of us. But it's just a wolf or a stupid lynx or a tasty deer. The humans get all excited and peer through the lens of their telescopes, but once again, no snow leopard.

"But we're there all right. As invisible as the snow, as inaudible as the night, as odorless as water. We swarm all around our admirers, those wusses in their fake coats of duck down. We laugh ourselves silly. We giggle. We chortle. We snicker. And we laugh at the other animals, too. Because even they don't notice us—until they end up in our clutches. They never live to tell the tale, though. That's why this presentation is about myself. Because we are unknown.

"I call us:


The emperors of the mountain tops.
The lords of the valley.
The mountain spirits of the white Cosmos.
We are invisible.
Untouchable.
Unbeatable.


"We are the best, the fastest, the strongest, the smartest, the most beautiful.

"Remember that.

"This was my presentation on the snow leopard. Are there any questions?"

"Yes. I have a question."

"Who are you?"

"The elephant."

"Never heard of you, but I'll listen."

"You've told us a lot about yourself, and I thank you for it. But I'm still missing some factual information."

"Factual information?"

"Yes, something we can verify."

"So what do you want to verify?"

"Where does it say that you're the strongest?"

"Do you doubt what I'm saying? You don't believe me?"

"I think you're beautiful and smart and fast, but I know a couple of species from my part of the world who are also very strong, maybe even stronger than you."

"Impossible. Who?"

"The rhinoceros, the hippopotamus, and myself, for example."

"Don't know any of them."

"It seems like you only know yourself."

"Any other questions?"

"Yes!"

"Who is yes?"

"Uh . . . the hazel dormouse."

"Don't know you either, but you sound too small to hunt."

"You've said a lot of nice things, but I don't really know where you live, what you eat, how big you are, or who your family is. Do you need water, for example? Do you climb trees? Do you live in a troop with other snow leopards? How are your young born and how do you raise them?"

"That's a lot of questions for a mouse. Just Google me. And don't forget to look at the pretty pictures. Some time ago a book about me was published, written by a famous French writer. The title—what else?—is *The Snow Leopard.* In it you can read everything I've told you here. All factual and true. Checked and double-checked.

"So that's it, this was my presentation about myself."

# 7

"AHEM. HE-HELLO.

"HELLO...YES. Let me start again.

"HELLO. I AM A HER...THE HER...
HER...Am I speaking too softly? Okay, then
I'll start again.

"HELLO, I . . . I'm very nervous. Pfffffffffffff.

"I'll start again. Sorry.

"HELLO. I AM A HERMOOT, no, I am a
hermate croo . . . No, let me start again.

"One, two, three . . . HELLO. I AM A HERMOTE. I am a hermite . . . hemereet . . . hookerite crab and my presentation today is on the, uh . . . the . . . what's it called again?

"Wait a minute . . . Sorry. I'll start again. Where was I? Oh, yes, back to the beginning.

"I AM A . . . CRABBY MITE, no, wait a minute . . . I really did practice this and it went just fine. But that was at home, in my shell. This is the most stressful thing I've ever done. Everyone is looking at me and I can't hide because I'm not allowed to give my presentation from inside my shell. Otherwise, it really would go well . . .

"So . . .

"One more time.

"*I AM A HAIRY CRAB*—oh, never mind. And my presentation today . . . I wish it was tomorrow, but it's today . . . my presentation today is on the uh . . . Yes, about a fish. It's blue. At least some of them are blue, because there are also yellow ones and purple ones and striped ones. There are those with dots and orange fins. There are so many colors. Black ones, too. Or green with a yellow tail, or yellow with a blue tail. Or brown with an orange back. Or purple with green on its head and yellow on its belly. Pink. Neon, pastel, rainbow. Some have stripes from top to bottom, or stripes from left to right or from right to left. They're so incredibly beautiful. That's why I'm giving my presentation on the, uh . . . that fish. I can't remember the rest. Any questions?"

"Yes. We actually know who *you* are, but we'd all like to know what animal you're talking about."

"Can I get back in my shell and shout it out?"

"Sure. It may lower your grade a little, but we really are very curious."

"Okay. Wait a minute while I go get my shell."

"We'll wait."

". . ."

"There, now I'm safe.

"I AM THE HERMIT CRAB
AND MY PRESENTATION
WAS ON THE REGAL BLUE TANG."

"Well, thank you. We thought it was very interesting."

"Any more questions?"

"No, but we do have some free advice and some big plus points."

"What are they, firefly?"

"Next time write down a few key words on a piece of paper and keep your shell within reach. And the plus points: when you started talking about the colors you were really on a roll. And not only that, but you're super brave."

"Oh . . . well . . . thank you all for listening and for the advice and the compliments. Unfortunately, my time is up. But the next time I'll tell you more about tangs, and the regal blue tang in particular— and yeah I'm gonna do it from my shell."

8

"HELLO,
I AM A MOLE
AND MY PRESENTATION
TODAY IS ON
THE DADDY LONG-LEGS.

"Daddy long-legs are insects with long legs. Six of them. Six legs and two wings that they use for flying, which they don't do very well. If the wind is blowing it carries the daddy long-legs along with it, which can be very annoying, so he clings to a tree or a nearby wall until the wind dies down.

"If a daddy long-legs finds that a bird has grabbed one of his legs, he just lets the leg go. He can live fine without it, since he can't walk very well either. Not even with all six legs. One leg more or less doesn't make much difference.

"Actually, the legs of the daddy long-legs aren't made for the long haul, since he doesn't have a lot of time to wear them out. His days are numbered as soon as he pops out of his cocoon.

"That's why the daddy long-legs doesn't have a mouth to chew with. He does have a proboscis—a sort of mouth—but it's pretty useless. His life is too short for a tasty meal. He's dead before he can work up an appetite.

"The daddy long-legs also can't sting like ordinary bugs. When you come right down to it, there's nothing that makes the life of a daddy long-legs even a little bit pleasant.

"So you might be thinking: Hey, mole, couldn't you have chosen a more interesting animal for your presentation? Like an okapi, or a penguin? Well, the truth is that the daddy long-legs is the best animal I know, loser or not. It's because of his babies—or rather, his larvae. They're incredibly tasty. The larvae of the daddy long-legs are called leatherjackets. They live half underground and half above the ground, and if I happen to bump into one, I eat every single bit of it, down to the last morsel. Those baby daddy long-legs are just sitting there, waiting for me to come along. Give me a serving of leatherjackets anytime. That should keep me going for a couple of hours.

"Leatherjackets look like fat, gray little worms that live on grass. So if humans want a nice green lawn in their yard, and there's a horde of leatherjackets munching on it, their best bet is to invite a couple of moles to get rid of them. Success guaranteed. No more yellow lawn.

"If a leatherjacket manages to survive a mole attack, and to escape the beaks of birds, he changes after a few months into a pupa. Inside the pupa the leatherjacket grows into a daddy long-legs. And once the daddy long-legs emerges from the pupa, he has only one thing on his mind: to make babies. Both the males and females basically start preparing my meal. Daddy long-legs are my chefs. Once they've finished their work, though, they can kick the bucket as far as I'm concerned. Their eggs are

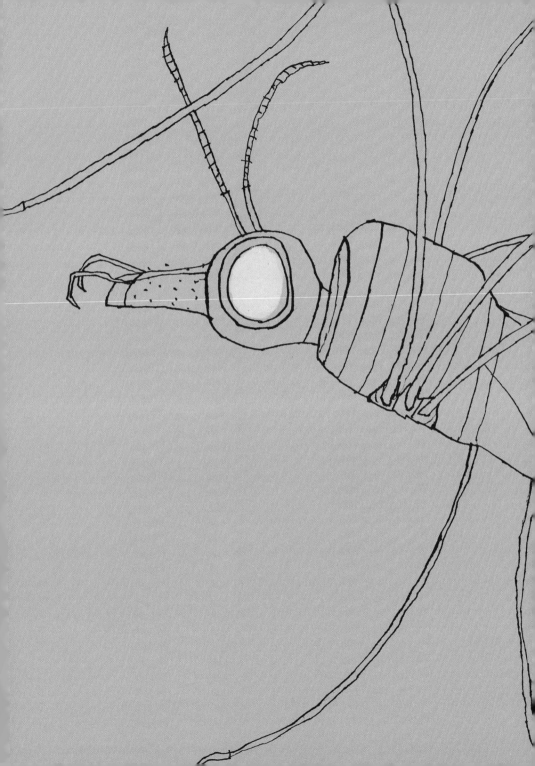

left to simmer in the grass, roasting in the sun with a splash of rain, until lots and lots of leatherjackets come crawling out. After that I have to wait patiently until they're big enough to go down my throat.

"So that was my presentation on the daddy long-legs. Are there any questions?"

"How many eggs does a daddy long-legs lay?"

"A couple of hundred all together in the grass. It could also be a thousand. As I always say, the more the better. Does anyone else have something to ask?"

"Yes. What do you mean by 'kick the bucket'?"

"Well, what I mean is: die. Pass away. Expire. Bite the dust. You get it, great spotted woodpecker? Or are you the middle spotted woodpecker? Or the lesser spotted woodpecker?"

"I'm the green one. The European green woodpecker."

"Whatever. We moles are as blind as bats anyway. But you get what I mean? After mating, daddy long-legs only live for a couple of days before they give up the ghost."

"I get it, and I eat leatherjackets too sometimes. But it does sound a little disrespectful, mole."

"We think so, too. We agree with the European green woodpecker."

"Who are you?"

"We're grubs, the children of the Maybug. It's disrespectful to talk about larvae that way. As if our only purpose in life was to be a snack for other animals."

"Well, that's what you are, aren't you? As a hedgehog, I totally agree with the mole."

"Yes. We starlings agree with the mole, too!"

"And so do the blackbirds!"

"And don't forget us crows. Wise words, mole!"

"We worms don't agree. On the contrary. We're on the leatherjacket and grub team."

"Ha-ha! Leatherjacket and grub team. Don't make us laugh. To us wild boars you're nothing but a juicy between-meal treat. We're on the mole team."

"That's not fair, you hogs!"

"Kids, kids, no fighting now."

"What do you mean, no fighting? Mind your own business, barn owl."

"Who's in charge here, anyway?"

"Nobody's in charge."

"Okay, calm down, everybody. This was my presentation. Next week it'll be your turn to pick an animal to talk about, daddy long-legs."

"But there's no point."

"What do you mean, there's no point?"

"You know what I mean. Next week I'll be . . . kicking the bucket."

"Oh. Right. Well, if it makes you feel any better, sooner or later we'll all be kicking the bucket. The Mayfly first, the tortoise last. That's the way nature designed it. Actually, I've worked up quite an appetite giving this presentation, so I'm going back underground. Thanks for listening. Toodle-oo!"

9

"HELLO,
I'M A FOX
AND MY PRESENTATION
TODAY IS
ON GEESE.

"There are lots and lots of geese. They come in all shapes and sizes. I'll mention just a few:

> graylag goose
> barnacle goose
> pink-footed goose
> snow goose
> Egyptian goose
> brant goose
> lesser white-fronted goose

"As far as I'm concerned, a goose is a goose. They're all equally tasty. They're easy to creep up on from behind, but be careful: if those birds happen to spot you, they make an enormous racket. You don't want to know about it. Geese are better at guarding than dogs. So it's advisable to hunt at dusk. They're less likely to notice you then.

"The goose's weak point is its neck. You just clamp your jaws around it. Then you shake it until its neck breaks, which means it's dead. Then you can drag it to your den. Geese look heavier than they actually are because they're fifty percent down.

"Then the tastiest part of the goose. That's the breast. The wings don't amount to much because you just end up with a mouthful of feathers. But the breast is t-e-n-d-e-r. Especially if the goose you've nailed is a young one, because young geese haven't flown very much and haven't developed a lot of muscle. Old geese are tough. That's because . . ."

"Hello. Can I ask you a few questions?"

"No, goose. I'm not finished yet."

"I don't agree with what you're saying."

"I'll hold a round of questions in a minute, and you'll be the first in line."

"Who's the head honcho around here anyway?"

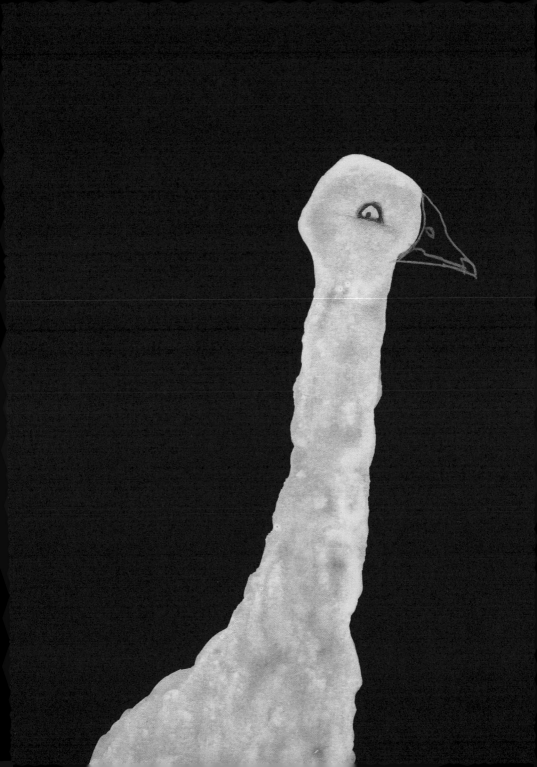

"Well, it's my presentation, so I'm the boss."

"And why should a goose listen to you?"

"Because you have to be polite, that's why."

"I don't think you're being very polite. You're only talking about us as meat."

"I only know you as meat."

"Well, I'm more than a drumstick, you know."

"Well, it's my presentation."

"Yeah, your presentation is about us as your next meal."

"If you don't mind, I'm going to continue. Where was I? Oh, yes. So what you need is a young goose. Old geese have already flown back and forth from Sweden to the Netherlands many times. Or from Russia to Germany or Belgium or Finland or somewhere else. Whatever. Geese spend winter in one place and summer in another. And the more often they've flown, the tougher their meat.

That's why I also go after the goslings. They make for tasty snacks if I happen to have a hungry litter myself. A baby goose fits right into the mouths of my cubs, and chewing on them is easy if all you've got is milk teeth."

"That's ENOUGH!"

"I'm just finished anyway. Any questions?"

"You bet!"

"So let's hear it."

"As a goose, I would like to know how you can sleep at night after all the murders you've committed of members of my family?"

"Well, let me put it this way: the more I murder the better I sleep."

"Then I'm giving you an F for your presentation."

"Why?"

"Because it's too one-sided."

"I agree with the goose."

"And who are you?"

"The vole."

"Ah, the vole, the tastiest snack on earth! Any more questions?"

"I'd like to say something. I think there was a lot more you could have said about geese. Such as their flights to the north. Why they do that. And how their extraordinary wingbeats work. That they basically pull each other through the air. And that they care for each other's young. Sometimes two geese care for at least thirty goslings at once. Ten of their own and the rest belonging to their friends. Why didn't you say anything about that, fox?"

"Because you, barn owl, are always such a know-it-all, and you're always poking your beak into everybody else's business. This presentation was about my interest in geese. And that interest has to do with meat."

"I think you could have done a bit more research on your prey."

"Research your own pellets, owl. This was my presentation. But you know what? You're right. And to make up for it I'm going to give next year's presentation on grass, that tasteless stuff that geese love so much. It'll be super short, that's for sure. Ha-ha-ha-ha-ha-ha!! Till then!"

10

"HELLO,
I'M AN EARTHWORM
AND MY PRESENTATION
TODAY IS ON
THE ANACONDA.

"Anacondas and earthworms look alike, and yet we're not. Actually, we're more unalike than alike, and that's the very reason why I think the anaconda is so awesome.

"I'm a worm and the anaconda is a snake. We can both wriggle, we don't have legs, and we slither along the ground. Our skin is smooth and we both prefer moisture to dryness. But that's where the similarities end.

"Worms drown if they go in the water, while the anaconda is a fantastic swimmer. He lives in the water most of the time, since he's much too heavy to crawl on the ground. He's the biggest snake in the world. Really super cool.

"Because he mainly lives in the water, his eyes are on top of his head. That's so he can look out across the water's surface. And his nostrils are on top of his nose. That's because his favorite food isn't fish, but land animals. He may have a heavy body, but underwater, he's almost weightless. And with his eyes and nose just above the water he can spy on the animals that are drinking along the bank, without being seen. His tactics make him invincible. I think he's super amazing.

"The females are twice as big as the males. That's because their young are born alive. Anaconda females don't lay eggs, like so many other snakes do. But when their pregnancy ends, up to eighty baby snakes crawl out of their belly—I repeat: eighty! And each one is longer than ten adult earthworms lined up head to tail.

"Some babies are even almost a yard long. Really cool. And that whole mass of live little snakes has to start hunting right away to get something to eat. After giving birth, their mother finally has room in her belly again for a whole deer, while her babies go and hunt mice and fish. Because newborn anacondas can crawl on land really well and they can also swim right away.

"Let me check my notes . . . oh, yes. Anacondas live in the South American rain forest. They're from the same family as the boa constrictor. Their skin is greenish brown with dark spots. They have no predators because they can take everybody on. I just think that's amazing. We worms have tons of predators, but there's nobody that anacondas can't beat. Their name means 'elephant killer.' So, that tells you plenty.

"That was my presentation. Anybody have questions?"

"Yes, I have a question for you. Is that okay?"

"Sure, let's have it, camel."

"When you say 'a baby anaconda is as long as ten earthworms lined up head to tail,' that can't be right."

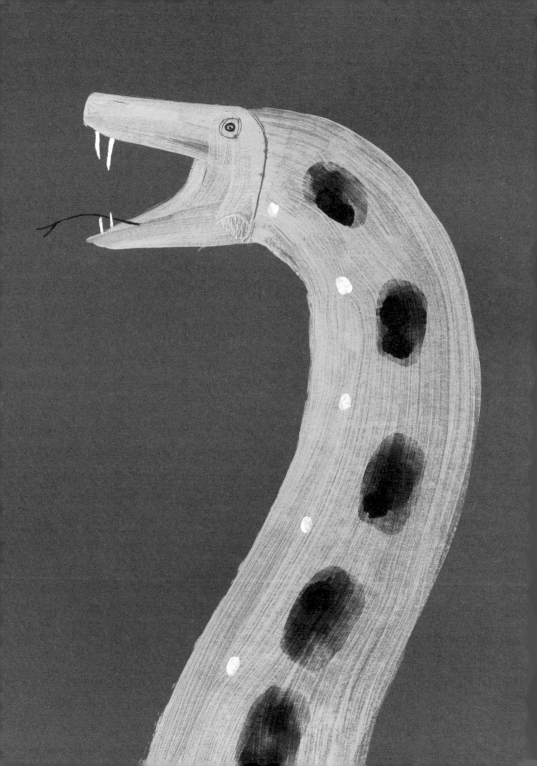

"Well, I mean approximately. If an earthworm is three inches long, and you multiply that times ten, you get thirty inches. That's about how long a newborn anaconda is."

"Yes, but that's not what I mean."

"So what do you mean, camel?"

"You worms can't line up head to tail."

"Why not?"

"Well, a snake has a head and a tail, but earthworms don't have a front or a back, right?"

"Then how do you think I'm talking, camel?"

"Uhhh . . ."

"We worms have a head and a mouth, so we also have a butt."

"Hi-hi-hi-hi-hi-hi."

"Who's giggling?"

"The edible dormouse. Hi-hi, you said 'butt.'"

"Oh, yeah, I mean my backside. Sorry for saying butt. What I wanted to say is, we worms certainly can line up head to tail."

"Thank you for your answer."

"You're welcome, camel. Any more questions?"

"Yes. How do anacondas kill their prey?"

"That's a good question, fox. Not like you do it, breaking their necks by shaking them, but by stran-gulation. Anacondas grasp their prey in their jaws. They don't use venom, but their teeth are very strong and sharp. Then the snake wraps his body all

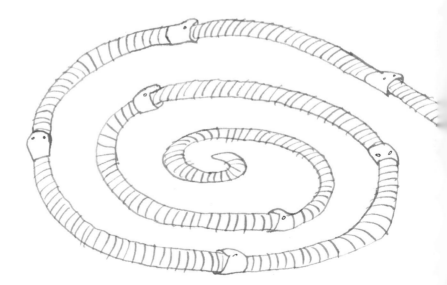

around the animal and crushes it, basically choking it to death. Then the anaconda opens his jaws wide. Wide enough for any animal to fit in. Wide enough for a deer, a capybara, a tortoise, or a sheep."

"Even a human?"

"That's what they say, but actually that never happens, fox."

"Too bad."

"Yes, too bad. I agree."

"Too bad. Right."

"We agree, too!"

"So do we!"

"I vote yes!"

"Come on, anacondas. You can do it!"

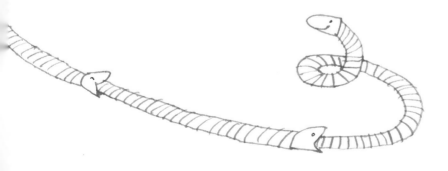

"Animals, animals, focus please. The worm was speaking."

"Thank you, barn owl. There once was a man who wanted to be eaten by an anaconda. Look it up. His name was—or *is*, because he's still alive—Paul Rosolie. An American. He wanted to know what it would be like to be gobbled up by a giant snake. He put on a protective suit and smeared himself with pig's blood. Inside his suit was enough oxygen for three hours, so he could breathe through a little tube once he got inside the snake's stomach. Then he and a camera team went in search of a big female anaconda. Animal lovers from all over the world were furious at him, because it was clear that the snake wouldn't survive. Even so, the guy went into the jungle. He let himself be attacked by a humongous anaconda. But once she wrapped her body around him and began to squeeze him tight, the guy started screaming bloody murder . . ."

"Coward!"

"Shhhh, fox. Let the worm finish his story."

"Thank you, barn owl. The whole world sympathized with the snake, because no one wanted such a beautiful animal to be cut open with a knife to save some stupid maniac. Excuse my choice of words."

"What a jerk!"

"Language, fox. Go on, worm."

"So the guy starts shouting that his arms were being pulled out of their sockets. But the anaconda didn't care, and she starts folding her jaws around his head. And then a whole group of men threw themselves on the anaconda and freed the guy. They say they didn't cause her any pain.

But to be honest, I think it was a vicious, mean experiment."

"Good presentation, worm."

"Thank you, fox. Any more questions?"

"Yes. Me."

"Go ahead, perch. Let's have it."

"Okay. I was just wondering: if the anaconda is invincible and he has no predators, why aren't there anacondas living all over the world?"

"Well, the anaconda can only live in swamps at just the right temperature, and you don't find those kind of habitats everywhere. And many of their young are eaten by caimans and birds. And the snakes that get old finally become weak or sick, and there are always piranhas lurking, or jaguars. And then it's curtains for the anaconda. They can live up to twenty years. But if I don't stop talking, we'll still be here in twenty years, and I don't have the time. Earthworms can last a few years, but not twenty. There's no time for any more questions. Thanks very much. This was my presentation on the anaconda."

## 11

"HELLO,
I'M A SOUTHERN
CASSOWARY
AND IN MY PRESENTATION
TODAY I'M DEALING WITH
THE HUMMINGBIRD.

"I only know the hummingbird from stories. Hummingbirds live on the other side of the world, way over in America, while I live in Australia. At first I thought the hummingbird was a fantasy bird. They look like butterflies with all those different colors. And they're so small. And they can fly so well. I can't fly at all. Birds like me are called flightless birds.

"There are many species of hummingbirds. My family consists of three species. I'm the southern cassowary. Then you have the dwarf cassowary and the northern cassowary. But when it comes to hummingbirds, there are a gazillion family members. Such as:

the speckled hummingbird
the emerald-chinned hummingbird
the purple-backed sunbeam
the ruby-throated hummingbird

the black-chinned hummingbird

the hyacinth visorbearer

the buff-tailed coronet

the fiery-tailed awlbill

the rufous hummingbird

the violet-headed hummingbird

the white-necked jacobin

the purple-collared woodstar

the green-crowned plovercrest

the olive-spotted hummingbird

the purple-bibbed whitetip . . .”

"Okay, southern cassowary. We get it. Can we ask some questions? Such as how small is the smallest hummingbird and how big is the biggest?"

"The smallest is about three inches and the biggest is eight inches, common ringed plover, but I do want to finish my list.

"You also have:

the white-tipped sicklebill
the sword-billed hummingbird
the mountain avocetbill
the tooth-billed hummingbird . . ."

"Southern cassowary, can I interrupt to ask you what they eat?"

"I'm getting to that, white-beaked dolphin."

"But . . ."

"Okay, but just this once: they eat nectar from flowers."

"Only nectar?"

"Yes, only nectar. And because they use so much energy for flying, they have to spend the whole day eating. Fly, eat, fly, eat.

"Now, where was I? Oh, yes:

the red-billed streamertail
the mountain velvetbreast
the broad-tailed hummingbird
the slender sheartail
the marvelous spatuletail
the bee hummingbird
the lucifer hummingbird
the giant hummingbird . . ."

"Cassowary, before you go on with your list, you said they can fly very well. What do you mean by that? Can they fly very high, or very fast, or very far?"

"They can fly straight up and straight down, Golfodulcean poison frog. They can fly forward and backward *and* they can hover, suspended in the air.

Just like a pied hoverfly, or a Batman hoverfly, or a marmalade hoverfly, or a European hoverfly, or a . . ."

"Okay, okay, we believe you. But why do hummingbirds hover?"

"I really have to get on with my list. But to answer your question: they hover in front of a

flower to suck out the nectar. Understand? Let's see. I've already mentioned the giant humming-bird . . . uh, oh yes:

the broad-tipped hermit
the Tolima blossomcrown
the many-spotted hummingbird
the blue-bearded helmetcrest . . ."

"Hey, are you from that family?"

"What do you mean, spotted hyena?"

"Well, you're a southern cassowary, and you're blue, and you've got a helmet, and you just men-tioned the blue-bearded helmetcrest."

"That's true, but just because you have similar features doesn't mean you're from the same family. There's also the helmeted guineafowl, the helmeted hornbill, and even the helmeted iguana. You don't think I'm from the same family as the iguana, do you?"

"No, but it's possible with that helmet on your head."

"You're not from the same family as the spotted python because you're a spotted hyena, right?"

"Uh . . . no, not really."

"And the Atlantic spotted dolphin isn't from the same family as the spotted python either, agreed?"

"What did you say about me?"

"Well, you're an Atlantic spotted dolphin, and you're not from the same family as the spotted python."

"Certainly not, southern cassowary."

"All right, then. I can continue . . ."

"Wait a minute. How do hummingbirds slurp their nectar? Do they have a straw attached to their beak? Is there something called a slurping hummingbird?"

"Ha-ha-ha-ha-ha-ha-ha-ha, that Golfodulcean poison frog is really funny!"

"Calm down, krill. No need to laugh at the cassowary."

"But we're not laughing at him. We just think the frog is funny, barn owl."

"Actually, what the hummingbirds do isn't slurping. It's licking."

"Licking?"

"Yes, they have a long, split tongue with little hairs all over it, and they use it to lick the nectar from the flower while they're flying."

"Thank you, cassowary. Go on with your list. You can skip the rest of the hoverflies."

"Ha-ha-ha-ha-ha-ha-ha-ha!"

"Shh. Focus, animals. Go on, cassowary. And don't let the krill bother you."

"Thank you, barn owl. I will continue:

the short-tailed woodstar
the slender-tailed woodstar
the glow-throated hummingbird
the black-backed thornbill
the white-tailed goldenthroat
the scissor-tailed hummingbird
the bearded mountaineer
the Antillean crested hummingbird . . ."

"You forgot something."

"What's that, Nathusius's pipistrelle?"

"You forgot to say hummingbird. You said scissor-tailed hummingbird, and after that you didn't say bearded mountaineer hummingbird, but only bearded mountaineer."

"Oh, that's true! Yes, you're right, I didn't. Not every species of hummingbird has the word hummingbird after its name. You can see that in many of the names I've listed. The short-tailed woodstar, for instance, and the black-backed thornbill. It's just the way hummingbirds get named."

"Okay, we're all finished now, southern cassowary. But we really enjoyed listening to you."

"When you say 'we,' do you mean all the animals really enjoyed listening?"

"Yes, 'we' means all the animals!"

"Including the hummingbirds themselves?"

"Yes, we hummingbirds had a great time hearing something about ourselves. Thank you, southern cassowary."

"You're welcome, animals, your applause is deeply moving. If I have forgotten any species—and actually I think I've forgotten the white-tufted sunbeam—I'll send an email."

"Not necessary, southern cassowary, don't trouble yourself. And we'll try to remember everything you said."

"Great! Then that was my presentation on hummingbirds."

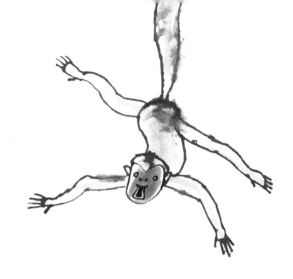

# 12

"HELLO
I'M A HOWLER MONKEY
AND MY PRESENTATION
TODAY IS ON
THE UNICORN.

"The unicorn is as big as an elephant.

"As heavy as a boulder.

"As white as an iceberg.

"As ferocious as the piranhas in the Amazon River.

"He's an animal with a built-in spear.

"He rushes his enemy and fills him with fear. He tears a hole in his belly as big as a coconut, whether it's a bear or a lion or a whale. Because he can also swim. He can cross the ocean, climb trees, and dig tunnels underground.

"He sleeps in the clouds during the day, but sometimes he sleeps at night, too, if he's tired from getting into fights. Or inflicting horrible bites.

"He loves islands. He can easily swim from Australia to Tierra del Fuego, or from Saba to Saint

Kitts, and from there to Komodo, where he slays the Komodo dragon. Because the Komodo dragon is stupid and the unicorn is smart.

"Once I saw a unicorn from my tree. He was traveling across the sky with another unicorn.

"I called out, 'Hey, unicorn!'

"And he called back, 'Hey, howler monkey.'

"I asked him, 'Where are you going?'

"He said, 'We're on our way to Bermuda.'

"I said, 'Are you going to take a dip in the Bermuda Triangle?'

"He said, 'Yes. It's monster wave season, so we're going there to play.'

"I said, 'Enjoy yourself, unicorn.

"He said, 'Thank you, howler monkey.'

"Once there was a unicorn who gored a great white shark. The shark was stuck on his horn so tight that the unicorn had to carry him around for a long time until the shark disintegrated. It was a real problem, because having a shark on his head meant that the unicorn couldn't see for weeks.

"Well, that was my presentation. Are there any questions?"

"I don't believe a word of it!"

"What don't you believe, starfish?"

"You made it all up."

"No, I didn't!"

"Yes, you did!"

"Who else thinks I made it all up?"

"All of us, howler monkey. There isn't a single animal who believes you."

"Oh, you don't believe me, do you? But you listened to me anyway."

"We were just being polite."

"That's right. We were being polite. And why did you start rhyming and then stop? You said spear and fear, and fights and bites."

"Sometimes you have to rhyme and sometimes you don't."

"So when do you rhyme and when don't you rhyme?"

"What kind of a question is that, leopard slug? Rhyming is something I decide for myself. I go by feel. It's my story and you all listened because for once it wasn't a boring presentation on hummingbirds and koalas."

"That's not fair. We could do the same thing, stupid howler monkey, and just invent something to talk about. You made it all up!"

"I didn't make anything up, hummingbird."

"So where does all the information about the unicorn come from then? Where did you find it?"

"What difference does it make?"

"If you give a presentation, the information has to make sense. You have to be able to say: 'I consulted such-and-such a book and checked such-and-such a website.'"

"Give me a break with your consulting and checking. I just consulted my brains. Which of the three hundred species of hummingbird are you, by the way?"

"I'm the sword-billed hummingbird."

"Ha-ha-ha-ha. Sounds like something the southern cassowary cooked up. If the unicorn doesn't exist, then you don't exist either, hummingbird."

"I certainly do exist. You can see me, can't you?"

"Your bill is as long as your body. Are you telling me that you can fit into an egg with a bill like that? And that you actually hatched from it? You were just put together in somebody's basement."

"Our bills don't grow until after we've crawled out of the egg."

"Well, the horn of a unicorn doesn't grow until he crawls out of his mother."

"But the unicorn doesn't exist. No one has ever seen one. And we do exist. That's the difference."

"Yeah, howler monkey. Your presentation is fake news. Fantasy. Made up. You get an F for effort."

"Keep out of this, starfish."

"Whoa, slow down, everybody . . ."

"Oh, no. It's the owl again. Okay, I did make it up. But you have to admit it was a good story, wasn't it, animals?"

"Yes, I thought it was a good story, howler monkey. I have one last question?"

"What's that, bitterling?"

"What animal rhymes with unicorn?"

"Okay, that's enough. This was my presentation. Bye-bye!"

# 13

"HELLO,
I'M A DEATH'S-
HEAD HAWKMOTH
AND MY
PRESENTATION
TONIGHT IS ON
THE SQUIRREL
MONKEY."

"Can we start with a question?"

"Of course. Go right ahead."

"Why do we have to listen to your presentation in the middle of the night?"

"Because I'm awake at night and I sleep during the day. I'm nocturnal."

"But we ordinary animals sleep at night. We're diurnal, and we're too tired to listen."

"We bats think nighttime is a perfect time."

"Yes, this is when we hedgehogs finally start thinking straight."

"Come on, everybody. Up until now the nocturnal animals have had to adjust to the diurnal animals. It's time we switched for once."

"Well said, barn owl. As if diurnal animals were better than nocturnal animals! I'm a nightjar and this has been bothering me for quite a while."

"Okay, animals. I'm going to start with my presentation.

"There's something strange about both of our names. I'm called a death's-head hawkmoth, because if you look carefully you can see the image of a skull between my wings. The squirrel monkey's entire head looks like a skull, but he's just called a squirrel monkey in English. In Dutch and German, though, he's called a death's-head monkey, like me. They call them squirrel monkeys in English because they're such good climbers, and they have long tails that they use to latch on to branches. Otherwise the squirrel monkey and I have nothing in common.

"I was once featured on the posters for a horror movie. The posters show a really big picture of a death's-head hawkmoth. Ever since then, people think I'm a horror creature."

"Can somebody please turn on the lights?"

"Go sit next to the barn owl if you're scared, sparrow. Then we can continue, because I think this presentation is really awesome."

"Thank you, fox. So there's this movie, a horror movie, and I have a role in it. The movie is really famous. But there's another movie in which a squirrel monkey plays a big role and that movie is famous, too. The difference is that since then I've become an animal that people are afraid of, while the squirrel monkey, with his death's-head face, has become a teddy bear. How crazy is that?"

"What are the names of the movies?"

"The horror movie is called *The Silence of the Lambs*. And the children's movie is about Pippi Longstocking. The squirrel monkey in that movie is called Mr. Nilsson, and he likes to sit on Pippi's shoulder."

"Forget Pippi for a minute, moth, and tell us about the serial killer."

"Pipe down, fox. Let's hear more about Pippi Longstocking."

"Aw, go sit on the barn owl's lap, sparrow, and have yourself a good cry."

"Focus, fox and sparrow. The death's-head hawkmoth is talking."

"Right. Let me continue. And if any of you want to know more about those movies, look it up yourselves."

"Good luck with doing that in the dark."

"Focus, animals! The death's-head moth has the floor."

"Okay. Where was I . . . A squirrel monkey eats fruit and insects. Fortunately, I live in Africa and Europe, so I'm not on Mr. Nilsson's menu.

Squirrel monkeys live in Bolivia, Peru, Suriname, and Brazil, which is basically the jungles of South America. They live in large groups so they can protect themselves from predators. And squirrel monkeys have lots of predators: snakes, jaguars, pumas, and birds of prey like the harpy eagle.

"The head of the group is a female. Actually, the whole group consists of females. Sometimes fifty monkeys or more. They're all grandmas, sisters, nieces, aunts, and granddaughters. They only let the males in if there are females who want to become pregnant. And once that happens, the males can go back home, wherever that is."

"I assume it's somewhere in a tree."

"Yes, sparrow, I think so, too. I'm glad you're still awake.

"When the boy monkeys are grown up they have to leave the female group. So they go off to join the males.

"As I said earlier, squirrel monkeys are really good climbers. Sometimes they pee on their hands, so when they climb through the branches the other monkeys will know who has been there.

"Well, I see it's starting to lighten up on the horizon. This was my presentation. I have time for one question. I can see you've been jumping up and down, sparrow, so what do you want to ask?"

"Well, what I wanted to know is: the squirrel monkey has a cute sort of name in English, but you're called a death's-head hawkmoth. They couldn't even call you a butterfly or something?"

"No, because I'm a moth."

"And you don't hurt anybody?"

"No, I can't sting and I can't bite."

"What would you rather be called, then?"

"That's a good question, sparrow. I'll spend the day sleeping on it."

"Sleep well, death's-head hawkmoth."

"Thank you all for listening. And have a restful day!"

# 14

"HELLO,
I'M A BARN OWL
AND MY
PRESENTATION
TODAY IS ON
THE TASMANIAN
DEVIL.

"I've been trying to decide what animal I should pick. At first, I thought about the barn swallow or the barn cat, or other animals that live in barns like horses or cows or even spiders—like Charlotte! But then I thought: let me take an entirely different approach. And that's why I'm going to say something about the Tasmanian devil."

"You always struck me as an old smarty-pants, barn owl, but I'm really looking forward to this."

"Nice, fox. Let me begin.

"The Tasmanian devil lives on an island that's part of Australia. The island is called Tasmania. Once there were Tasmanian devils living on the Australian mainland, but they disappeared thousands of years ago.

"This animal is named after the devil, but actually there's no connection between the two. When the first Europeans went to explore the island of Tasmania, they heard such terrifying noises coming from the forest that they thought the devil lived there. All that shrieking made the newcomers want to turn right around and go home. Because no one wants to come face-to-face with the devil, believe me. Not now, not four hundred years ago. Humans get very nervous when it comes to that sort of thing.

"When the men discovered where the sound was coming from, it wasn't the devil they saw, but a small animal the size of a cat. It looked like a little bear, but it wasn't a bear. It turned out to be a marsupial, just like the koala. The midwife toad has already told us about the koala.

"But unlike the koala, the Tasmanian devil isn't a marsupial that eats the leaves of trees, but a marsupial that spends the whole day eating meat. His jaws are stronger than those of any mammal of the same size. So the lynx and the wolverine and the Norwegian

Forest cat don't stand a chance with their teeth and fangs: The grip of a Tasmanian devil's jaws is much stronger than theirs. That's because his head is huge compared to the rest of his body. He can rip the skin off a kangaroo with the greatest of ease, and break the bones of a wallaby as if they were twigs."

"Go on, barn owl. This is super awesome."

"Well, as a koala it makes me a little nervous."

"Don't worry, koala. Tasmanian devils don't climb trees. The young ones do, but they wouldn't attack a koala. Besides, there are no koalas in Tasmania, and there are only a handful of devils on the Australian mainland. But I'll get back to that later.

"The Tasmanian devil lives alone, but if there happens to be something to eat all the devils come rushing out of the forest together. Say there's a dead kangaroo lying on the roadside. The devils will dive onto the carcass like they haven't eaten in weeks.

While they're eating, they shriek like seagulls, roar like lions, snort like buffaloes, and groan like trees in a storm. They squeak like rats and snarl like cats. And they do that to frighten each other off. To avoid fighting. But there's still quite a bit of fighting anyway. Sometimes the devils look even more battered than the carcass they've been feasting on. Full of wounds and blood."

"Oh, stop. This is making me sick."

"Shut your beak, goose. I'm really getting into this. Go on, barn owl. I never knew there was such a good storyteller lurking under that suit of silky feathers."

"I think it's a cool story, too."

"You see? The shark agrees with me, so don't let that dumb goose distract you."

"Watch your mouth, fox, but I'm glad you can appreciate what I have to say.

"So Tasmanian devils are real scrappers. They kill each other while they're eating together, which they also do when the males are looking for females. Not only do the males tear into each other, but they also attack the females, oddly enough. During mating season, when babies are being made, the females deliberately get heavier and fatter so they can resist the bites of their men. Personally, I find this a very strange state of affairs."

"So do I."

"You stay out of this, rabbit. Go on, barn owl, take your time."

"So finally the females become pregnant—from several different males at the same time, by the way—and if they survive all that mating, they quickly give birth to about thirty young. These babies are very small. A quarter of an inch long. As long as a mouse's leg—no, shorter—as long as an ant's antenna. There's just one big problem: the mother only has four nipples in her pouch. So she can only nurse four babies, and no more. That means that twenty-six of the thirty young will die.

"So each birth marks the beginning of a frantic life-or-death race. Thirty naked little pipsqueaks have to get to a nipple as soon as they can. The first young perish on the way to the pouch. The rest die at the entrance.

"Only the four strongest babies find a nipple. They clamp right on and start sucking—just like with the koalas—and slowly grow over the weeks that follow. In the end, only one of the young, maybe two, reach adulthood. And the female produces only three or four young during her lifetime because she only lives to be five or six years old. Tasmanian devils have a hard life, but they have a wild time while they're at it. That's something we owls are a

little jealous of, I guess. Well, that was my presentation. Questions, anybody?"

"Yes. I have a question."

"Let's hear it, fox."

"I'd like to know who the predator of the Tasmanian devil is."

"That's a good question. The fact is, things are not going well for the Tasmanian devil. At first there were lots of them, but now there are only about twenty-five thousand. That's because of a deadly disease that's spreading among their species. It's a contagious form of cancer—facial cancer, to be exact. It spreads by means of wounds, which is exactly what devils inflict on each other: bite wounds.

"Tumors first form on the devils' snout and then grow into their mouth. Their teeth fall out, they can't chew anymore, and finally they starve. So, the Tasmanian devil seems to be making itself extinct.

"But there's good news. For some time now, little devils have been born who recover from facial cancer or don't even become infected. It looks like they're going to overcome the disease. Is that an answer to your question, fox?"

"Absolutely. Thank you."

"Are there any other questions?"

"You told me you were going to say something else about devils on the Australian mainland, where I happen to live."

"Oh, yes. You're right, koala. Good thing you reminded me. Researchers wanted to keep Tasmanian devils from going extinct because of that horrible disease, so they released a group of healthy animals onto the Australian mainland."

"Noooooo!"

"Wait a minute, koala. It was only twenty-six. Now, there are a hundred, but as I've already told you they don't climb trees. The researchers released them into a large area surrounded by a fence. For that reason, they first removed the wild cats and foxes—"

"Noooooo!"

"Take it easy, fox. They removed the cats and foxes as a precaution. How did they do it? I don't know. But the researchers didn't want the devils to be attacked by cats and foxes. Cats and foxes are not native to Australia. They were brought there by humans, just like the rabbits. They don't belong there either. The researchers wanted to protect the Tasmanian devils from that dreadful disease and from predatory animals. They just wanted to be on the safe side. This marsupial cannot be allowed to go extinct. They enrich our world. So that was my presentation. Thank you for listening."

## 15

"HELLO,
I'M A LEAF INSECT
AND TODAY I WANT TO
GIVE A PRESENTATION ON
THE SEA ANEMONE."

"That's not allowed!"

"Why isn't it allowed, hummingbird?"

"Because these presentations are only supposed to be about animals, and anemones are plants."

"Yes, but in the water they're animals."

"Yeah, hum . . . yeah, huh-huh-hum . . ."

"Crawl into your shell, hermit crab."

"Thank you. What I wanted to say is: that's right. Anemones are animals."

"Thanks for your two cents, hermit, and *please* stay in your shell, for heaven's sake. As far as I'm concerned there's no need for you to come out again."

"None of us think you ever have to come out again."

"Thank you, animals. Then I'll stay in my shell from now on, unless I outgrow it."

"Okay, so I'll continue with my presentation. Sea anemones live underwater. They can be found all over the ocean and there are lots of different species.

"Many people think that sea anemones are plants. I myself am often mistaken for a plant. Or part of a plant. I look so much like the leaf of a tree that the species I belong to is called 'leaf insect.'

"There are also insects called walking sticks, and they look a lot like twigs. Maybe they should have called the sea anemone a 'walking anemone,' to avoid confusion. Because they can walk, sort of, although it looks more like shuffling. They don't walk on six legs, like us insects, but on one foot. And the sea anemone doesn't walk very often, because once he's found a nice comfortable spot, he isn't likely to move.

"The sea anemone belongs to the class called 'anthozoa,' which means 'flower animal.' Another example of a flower animal are corals. And they're from the same family as the jellyfish. Jellyfish have tentacles just like sea anemones, which they use for catching food. And both species have only one entrance and exit. So the food goes in through a mouth and the poop comes out through the same mouth. Some animals think that's weird, but there are lots more animals that use the same opening for different things."

"Yuck. Which ones?"

"Well, how about yourself, hummingbird?"

"Huh?"

"Birds pee and poop through the same opening, which is where the eggs of the female birds also come out."

"That's different."

"Yes, but I just wanted to say that we all have something that others don't understand."

"Wise words, leaf insect."

"Thank you, barn owl."

"Can I ask what there is about you that others wouldn't understand? I mean, you just said we all have something that others wouldn't understand, so what is that in your case?"

"Let's save that for the end, okay, hummingbird?"

"That's fine. I'm just curious, leaf insect."

"Now let's see. Oh, yes. When an anemone finds a good spot, he attaches himself to the ocean floor by means of suction. And if there's sand on the ocean floor, he digs himself in. He uses his tentacles to try to catch food. A small fish, a shrimp—whatever passes by. There are little poisonous harpoons in his tentacles, which he uses to paralyze his prey.

"The more an anemone eats, the more tentacles he makes. And the more tentacles he has, the more food he can catch. That's unique in the animal

kingdom, because there's no other animal that gets more arms if he eats more."

"So he really does have something in common with a plant."

"You're right, reindeer, because a healthy plant with enough light and water also grows more branches. In fact, sea anemones can feed on light too, just like plants. Light is really important to them, because without light a sea anemone would die.

"So that was my presentation. Are there any questions?"

"Yes, how old can a sea anemone get?"

"Gosh, I don't exactly know. Good question, worm."

"Can I answer that one?"

"Of course, hermit crab."

"A sea anemone can live to be sixty-five years old."

"Wow, that's old. Thanks for the answer. Any more questions?"

"Yes. If the sea anemone is so poisonous, who are his predators?"

"Good question, fox. I don't exactly know. But maybe the hermit crab does."

"Well, the sea anemone's biggest predator is the sea slug. Sea slugs aren't a bit put off by those tentacles. And can I tell you something else?"

"Sure, hermit crab."

"Well, we hermit crabs sometimes live with sea anemones, which is why I know so much about them. Instead of attaching itself to a stone, the sea anemone attaches itself to our shell. It looks like we're wearing a hat. We sort of drag the sea anemone across the ocean floor. That makes us hermit crabs feel safer, because our predators are afraid of the sea anemone's poisonous tentacles. After we've been hunting, we hermit crabs leave a bit of our prey for the sea anemones as a way of thanking them for their protection. That gives them something to eat as well. A bit of protection in exchange for a meal, you might say."

"Nicely explained, hermit crab. Do you have a question, hummingbird?"

"Yes. You were going to tell us something about you that others wouldn't understand."

"Oh, right. What is it about me that you wouldn't understand? Well, our predators are insect eaters. That's logical, since we're insects. But there are also herbivores who are dangerous to us. Herbivores are animals who like to eat leaves, and sometimes they accidentally take a bite out of us and then spit us out. Herbivores don't understand that we're not leaves, but insects. They commit accidental murder, which is why we have to watch out for walking sticks. They love leaves. On the other hand, we would never take a bite out of a walking stick, even though we like to eat insects. A walking stick is an insect, but it doesn't look like one. If we come across a walking stick, we leaf insects say to ourselves: Oh, a twig, let's look for something juicier. Ha-ha-ha-ha! You see how that works?"

"Yes, we see how it works. I thought it was a great presentation."

"Thanks for the compliment, mole cricket. And thank you, hermit crab, for your help."

"You're welcome, leaf insect. It was fun helping you."

"So that was my presentation. Thank you all for listening."

16

"HELLO,
I'M THE WHITE RHINOCEROS
AND TODAY I'M GIVING
MY PRESENTATION ON
THE SHOEBILL.

"I'm keeping this close to home. We both live in Africa. We don't get in each other's way, the shoebill and I, but we do have a lot in common. If you're wondering how a rhinoceros can have anything in common with a bird, I'm here to tell you: it's possible.

"So.

"That's why.

"The shoebill is a name that humans came up with because they think his bill looks like a shoe, which is a thing we animals don't need. So why give such a name to a bird? It's like my name: they call me a white rhinoceros, even though I'm not white. And the black rhinoceros isn't black. But that's not what my presentation is about.

"So.

"There's that.

"The shoebill looks strong and gray. Just like me. But with a bill. A bill that has a hook at the end.

I have a horn on my snout. Our heads look prehis-
toric, as if we were around when the world began.
But we weren't. It looks that way though.

"So.

"That, too.

"We're both threatened with extinction.
People stop when they see us. Either to shoot us or
to admire us. Unfortunately, they'd rather shoot us.

"That's why.

"The shoebill sometimes stands stock-still for
half a day just to catch something. I move slowly,
too, just like the shoebill.

"There's that.

"If the shoebill sees a fish or a small alligator,
he pounces. First his bill, then his whole body. Right
into the water. Headfirst. Hits the target most of the
time. But he's big. Not as big as me, but big for a
bird. More than three feet tall. Bet on it.

"The male and the female care for their young together. When they can see which of the young is strongest, they ditch the rest. They just don't feed them. It's brutal, but it's their decision. Not mine.

"Any questions?"

"Yes, is he in the same family as any other birds? The stork, for example? The stork is also a big bird."

"No."

"What do you mean, no? That he's not in the same family as the stork?"

"Exactly."

"So is he in the same family as the heron, or the flamingo?"

"There is no family, anteater."

"Okay, thank you."

"Any more questions?"

"I thought he was a distant relative of the pelican?"

"Then you thought wrong, water flea."

"Not exactly the same family, but sort of, I mean."

"No such thing as sort of, water flea. The shoebill belongs to the family of the shoebills. And that family has only one member. No more and no less. But there's also an order. The shoebill belongs to the order of the pelecaniformes. And that order has four other families. It's that simple."

"Which families then?"

"Okay, water flea. You get the whole list. The pelecaniformes is comprised of the following families:

1. herons
2. pelicans
3. hamerkops
4. ibises and spoonbills
5. shoebills"

"Thank you, rhinoceros."

"I'm not finished, water flea. Those five families all belong to the same order but that doesn't mean they're from the same family. By way of comparison! My own family consists of five species. I'll list them for you:

1. white rhinoceros
2. black rhinoceros
3. Sumatran rhinoceros
4. Javan rhinoceros
5. Indian rhinoceros

"We're all family. So.

"And my entire family, all five species together, also belongs to an order: the order of the odd-toed ungulates. I'm not going to list all the families in that order. But another family in the order of the odd-toed ungulates are the equids: the horse family. Well, you can't say that equids like zebras and wild donkeys are from the same family as mine. So the shoebill is not from the same family as the pelican either. They belong to the same order, but not the same family. Got it?"

"I think so, rhinoceros. Thank you."

"Any more questions?"

. . .

"No? Then that was my presentation. So."

# 17

## "HELLO, I'M A GILA MONSTER, AND TODAY..."

"What? Who are you?"

"I'm a Gila monster. And today . . ."

"Forget about today. *Never*, you mean. Get out of here!"

"Yeah, the quail is right! Get out of here, Gila monster!"

"But . . ."

"You're dangerous!"

"Yes, way too dangerous!"

"But how about the snow leopard? And the fox? They're much more dangerous than I am, aren't they?"

"No, they're not!"

"Yes, they are. They eat a whole lot more meat than I do, and they were allowed to give their presentations."

"Yes, but you have the breath of death."

"Who says?"

"That's what we've heard. When you exhale, everybody around you gets poisoned. You don't even have to bite them."

"Exactly! Anyone who gets within fifteen feet of you is a goner."

"We've even heard that you're fatal at three hundred feet."

"At two miles even. Check it out."

"One breath from your lair and nobody has a prayer. That rhymes; it must be true."

"But I don't even live in a lair."

"Doesn't matter. You've got to go."

"But you're all still alive, and I've been breathing in and out all this time! Poison breath doesn't exist. I'm not a dragon. Anyway, my presentation is on . . ."

"But you are a monster."

"Yes, you're a monster and that's why you have that name."

"Animals, it's an old wives' tale. People used to say that about me, but it's not true. I would never poison anyone from a distance. Why would I do such a thing?"

"Because you're a monster, a Gila monster!"

"I'm not a monster. I'm a beaded lizard—a heloderma suspectum."

"Ah-ha! Suspectum! I suspected as much."

"Heloderma. What's that mean?"

"Uh . . . skin like the head of a nail."

"Holy cow! That's even worse."

"Whoa. Before we know it, you'll start shooting nails at us."

"They're not really nails. I just ended up with a misleading name. They're little bone-like balls

under my skin, and I can't shoot anything at anybody. In fact, my skin falls off sometimes as I grow."

"Ew!"

"Yes, but all animals lose something some-
time. Birds molt. They get new feathers. Animals
with fur molt, too. And snakes get a new skin. Take
that anaconda, for instance, that you all thought was
so cool."

"Yeah, but the anaconda doesn't poison anyone. He only strangles them."

"Listen. There are other snakes that are much
more poisonous than I am, like the rattlesnake or
the cobra. Not to mention the black mamba. I only
use my poison for self-defense."

"But you do have poison in your jaws."

"That's only to defend myself, I'm telling you.
And I don't have poisonous teeth for injecting it into
my victim. The poison comes out of my lower jaw.

From a gland. That's different. And if I bite, yes, there is some poison involved. But only if I'm being attacked."

"But once you bite someone you don't let go."

"Well, that's just how it works, gerbil."

"You suddenly appear out of nowhere. You grab whatever gets in the way of your jaws."

"No, that's absolutely not true. Good grief, animals, it's time somebody did a presentation on me because you really have the wrong idea about Gila monsters. You've all been misinformed, as they say."

"We can tell from your gory colors that you're super poisonous. That yellow and pink are blinding us."

"But quail, I spend ninety percent of my time underground, in a little burrow. I only venture out in the morning."

"Yeah, to hunt for us."

"I'm one of the slowest lizards in the world. I crawl along, step by step. I can't even run."

"No, no. You hunt buffaloes and wolves, that's what we heard."

"Who from?"

"What difference does it make? We just know it's true."

"I can't go after prey because I'm way too slow. Really."

"What do you eat then, liar?"

"I eat eggs, because they don't run away."

"You eat our unborn children!"

"Yes, that's true. And I also eat young birds and young mice and rats that are still in the nest. I have no choice."

"You're a monster!"

"Sorry, animals. Excuse me for living. I didn't mean to scare you, but my eggs sometimes get eaten, too, you know. I only lay twelve, and they take a really long time to hatch. Almost ten months. So I take up less space on earth than other animals do."

"Even so, we don't want you around."

"Fine, if that's what you really want, I'm leaving. I'm out of here. Sorry. No problem. See you later—or maybe never."

"Yeah, get lost, and never come back!"

"Well, he's gone."

"Good job, everybody. We came that close to being poisoned."

"You're so right, yellow scorpion. We escaped by the skin of our teeth."

"Does anybody know what the presentation was about?"

"You mean the Gila monster's presentation?"

"Yes, what was he going to talk about?"

"No idea, quail. Do you know, barn owl?"

"No, we didn't give him enough time to tell us. He began talking, but then somebody cut him off."

"Actually, we're all pretty curious."

"Can't he submit his presentation in writing?"

"That's what I'd like to do next time, a written presentation. A kind of essay, if you know what I mean."

"Yeah, we get it, hermit crab."

"I feel kind of sorry for him. He was actually a nice guy. He didn't hurt anybody. And we hermit crabs also eat shrimp—I mean, live animals. And

161

there are seagulls that eat us. In the end we all eat each other."

"Not true, hermit crab!"

"Who said not true?"

"We did! We plankton wouldn't hurt a fly."

"Animals, animals, let's take a vote."

"Vote about what, barn owl?"

"Vote about giving the Gila monster a second chance."

"No way!"

"Never!"

"Out of the question!"

"Forget it!"

"Not a chance!"

"We vote against it, too."

"I vote for it!"

"I vote with the hermit crab."

"So do I!"

"If his breath really was poisonous, we'd all be sick by now. And none of us got sick. He didn't bite anyone, either. And did you see how he walked away? A tortoise walks faster than that. So a lot of the stuff that's said about him must be hogwash. And that's really mean."

"I ate one once."

"What did you say, coyote?"

"Well, I ate a Gila monster once. They're easy to catch. You have to watch out for their mouth, but otherwise, they make a hearty meal."

"Yuck, that's gross."

"No, it's not. The coyote is right. We golden eagles also get the occasional Gila monster in our claws."

"Animals, I propose that we give the Gila monster a second chance. We haven't treated him fairly. Who's going to bring the Gila monster back?"

"I'll give it a try."

"Good, hermit crab. And thank you for speaking up for him."

"Yes, thank you, hermit crab. We're all proud of you."

"Take your shell with you, for when you get close. Ha-ha-ha-ha-ha!"

"Shut up, fox."

"That's enough, animals. Who's up next?"

"I am."

"Aha, the wild donkey. Would you switch places with the Gila monster? It's going to be awhile before he gets back."

"Yeah, he's not much of a walker, ha-ha-ha."

"Fox! Enough! Thank you, wild donkey. You're a good sport."

"I have to do a little practicing, barn owl, but then I think I'll be ready."

"Let us know when that is. What animal will you be talking about? We can start looking forward to it."

"It's a presentation on the megabat."

# 18

"Hello, is it my turn?
Or is the Gila monster
on his way?
No?
Should I begin then?

"Good.
I'm a wild donkey
and my presentation
today is on
megabats.

"I just chose any old animal because I couldn't make up my mind. I started with A, and then came B and C. And before I knew it, I was already up to V. And finally there was Z, and I would be having to give my presentation on the zebra. Not that I don't like zebras, but I live in Africa, not far from them. What if I said something wrong? Besides, somebody has already given a presentation on the zebra."

"That's right!"

"You see? You should never repeat what's already been done."

"It was a lousy presentation about us anyway. It would have been okay with me, wild donkey."

"Who gave that presentation?"

"A human."

"A human? About you?"

"Yes. She compared me to a bar code. No idea what that is, but it sounds . . . how shall I put this?

Disrespectful. And what she said about my stripes was a hundred percent wrong."

"Then let's bar that human from our presence, zebra."

"Ha. Yes, let's do that, wild donkey. I'm eager to hear what you have to say about megabats."

"Yes, so are we! Take it away, wild donkey."

"Good. The megabat looks like a bat, but you shouldn't confuse the two. They come from very different families. The bat has a tail and the mega-bat doesn't. Most bats have sonar to keep them from flying into things and to track down prey. A megabat doesn't even know what sonar is—which is lucky, because then I don't have to explain how sonar works.

"There are many species of megabats, and they live in lots of different places in warm

countries. The biggest species is sometimes called the flying fox. The fox ought to like that, right, fox?"

"Absolutely, wild zebra. Super cool. What does he eat? I mean: who are his victims?"

"Well, fox, first of all . . . I'm a wild donkey, not a wild zebra. And second, you'd probably find his menu disappointing, because megabats lick the nectar and pollen from flowers and they eat fruit. Nothing bloody about their meals. They don't sink their teeth into the flesh of an animal like you do— and like some bats do, too. No, the megabat prefers to sink his teeth into a banana.

"But let's take a look at the scientific name of the flying fox: Pteropus vampyrus. It's kind of strange, because a last name like that really makes you think of something bloody. Vampyrus was thought up by humans, and what do they know about animals? Next to nothing. We're slowly coming to realize that. Look at that presentation the human gave on the zebra. A big fat F. No, a flying fox doesn't drink blood. He eats fruit. He's what they call a frugivore."

"A what?"

"A frugivore."

"What's that, if I may ask?"

"That, sloth, is an animal that lives on fruit. Like many birds and some monkeys."

"And what am I then?"

"A sloth is an herbivore. You eat leaves and stuff like that."

"And me?"

"You're an omnivore, fox. You eat everything. Berries, birds, whatever comes your way."

"And us?"

"You tigers are real carnivores. Carnivores are meat eaters. Just like sharks and crocodiles and, uh . . . barn owls."

"And what are you, wild donkey?"

"I eat plants, so I'm an herbivore, like the sloth."

"Nice to know, wild donkey."

"Thank you, sloth. So let me continue.

"Megabats come in all different sizes, from small to big. The biggest species, the flying fox, has a wingspan of almost six feet."

"Yikes!"

"Take it easy, fox. Do you have to comment on everything?"

"Yeah, fox, shut it."

"Megabats sleep during the day and hunt for food at night. And because humans—those stupid humans again—have been chopping down the trees in the jungle and planting banana trees in their place, the flying foxes have taken to hanging out in the banana trees for a tasty dessert. Which makes the humans angry, because they think the trees belong to them and not to the animals. What a dumb species. So they shoot the megabats out of the trees.

"Boom! Plop! Dead!

"The humans say: We planted the trees, so the megabats have to shove off. But the trees that were there before the banana trees really did belong to the megabats and the other animals. So I think it's ridiculous, if you want my opinion."

"Yes, we do. We think it shouldn't be allowed. It's robbery!"

"I think it's criminal. There you are, a happy sloth hanging in your tree, and along comes the human with his ax."

"Yeah, or a saw. Then out you tumble, coconut and all."

"It's murder!"

"Yes, it is. Tree murder, which also means megabat murder."

"And sloth murder."

"And orangutan murder."

"It's animal murder!"

"Animals, animals, focus please."

"But barn owl, *we're* the focus. You can't get any focuser than us."

"You're right, maned wolf. For the first time we all agree. Right?"

"Yes! One for all and all for one!"

"Well, personally, I don't much care what the human does. I mean, I suck human blood, deer blood, hedgehog blood. Whatever."

"Great, there's the tick again. The most ineradicable animal on earth."

"Now, now. We don't discriminate here, fox. An animal is an animal is an animal."

"Yeah, and a wild donkey is a megabat is a barn own. Give me a break! All animals are not alike. A tick is just super inferior."

"I'll get you in the lip someday, fox, then you'll sing a different tune."

"Be my guest, tick. You bite me once and you're more or less dead, with that squishy, blood-soaked body of yours . . ."

"May I please finish my presentation on the megabat? What I still wanted to say is that flying foxes, like all other megabats, are nocturnal animals. When they do go to sleep, during the day, they wrap themselves up in their big wings like the rind of an orange. Then they hang that way all together, upside down, from the branches of a tree. It's a beautiful sight—as if the flying foxes had become fruit themselves.

"So that was my presentation. Any questions?"

"Yes!"

"Ask away, fox."

"Well, I think your name is really cool. Can any animal add 'wild' to their name? I'd love to be called wild fox."

"No idea. There's the wild duck and the wild horse. So I would say, go ahead, knock yourself out. Any more questions? No? Then that was my presentation. Thank you all for listening."

# AFTER A LONG WAIT...

"Does anybody know if the hermit crab is on his way with the Gila monster?"

"Nobody's heard anything yet, barn owl."

"Giraffe, can you see anything?"

"No, nothing on the horizon."

"Did the hermit crab take his shell with him, by any chance?"

"Yes, of course, rhinoceros. He wouldn't dare go anywhere without it."

"How about I fly out to meet them?"

"Good idea, rose-ringed parakeet."

"What do you mean, meet them? You don't even know if they're on their way back, do you?"

"Not so negative, mole. Go back underground and do your moping there."

"I'll mope wherever I want, cleaner fish."

"Animals, pay attention. We're almost at the end of this series of presentations, so let's keep it pleasant. I propose that the rose-ringed parakeet goes out to investigate."

"Since when did they put you in charge, barn owl?"

"I think it just sort of happened, snow leopard. If you all want someone else to take over, that's fine with me, of course."

"So let's take a vote."

"And naturally you'll vote for yourself, right snow leopard?"

"Absolutely, howler monkey."

"Animals, animals, let's not get sidetracked. We'll just wait and see what happens. In the meantime, maybe someone else can give their presentation?"

"Yes, me!"

"Who?"

"Me!"

"Where are you?"

"Here!"

"Where?"

"On the strawberry."

"I don't see any strawberry."

"The strawberry plant on the ground under the beech tree!"

"That I can see, but where are you?"

"On the strawberry, the one that's already a little rotten."

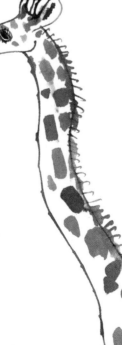

"Aha, there you are. Welcome, fruit fly."

"Thank you, barn owl."

"So, what's your presentation going to be about?"

"I'll tell you that when I start."

"Okay, fruit fly. The floor is yours!"

19

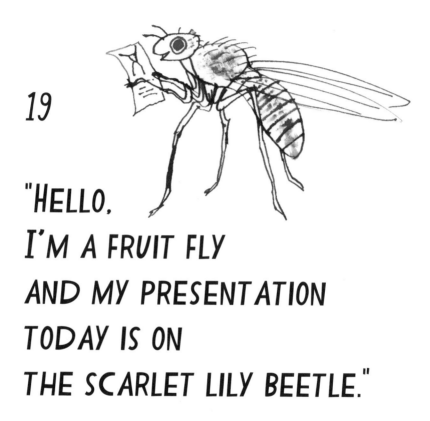

"HELLO,
I'M A FRUIT FLY
AND MY PRESENTATION
TODAY IS ON
THE SCARLET LILY BEETLE."

"Take it away, shorty!"

"Yeah, looking good, fruit fly."

"Are you a frugivore?"

"Ha-ha-ha-ha-ha! Who said that about a
frugivore?"

"I did!"

"We should have known. The fox again with
his bad jokes."

"Let's let the fruit fly get started, animals."

"Actually, the fox is right. I am a frugivore.
There's nothing I wouldn't do for a nice piece of
fruit. And because I especially love strawberries,
I thought I'd talk about a red animal. That's how I
came up with the scarlet lily beetle. And you guessed
it: the scarlet lily beetle loves lilies. Delicious,
according to him. The leaves of the lily plant in
particular.

"The scarlet lily beetle never used to be so common. But when humans began sending lilies all over the world to add to bouquets, the scarlet lily beetle just hitched a ride with his dinner, and now they live almost everywhere. Wherever humans love lilies, really. Unfortunately, it's mainly the flowers that humans love and not the animals that live on them. Although to be honest (and this is my teensy-weensy fruit fly opinion), I think the scarlet lily beetle is prettier than the whole plant put together.

"Scarlet lily beetles come from the family of leaf beetles. The strange thing is that I could never find out where the scarlet lily beetle originally came from. Somewhere in Asia, somewhere in Europe. But that sounds much too vague. Apparently, no one wants to admit that the scarlet lily beetle is one of them and they're proud of him. No, all the things I've read say he accidentally arrived with the lilies.

Like vermin. Everybody points to everybody else. 'He comes from your neck of the woods.' 'No, from yours.' So what? What difference does it make where you come from? But what do I know? I'm just a fruit fly, so my opinion isn't that important."

"Everybody counts, fruit fly!"

"Thank you, death's-head hawkmoth.

"So I don't where scarlet lily beetles come from, but what I do know is that now they live everywhere, and I think they're gorgeous.

"The scarlet lily beetle is blazing red, which makes him stand out. That's why he eats mostly from the underside of the lily leaf, so it's harder for his predators to see him. He doesn't have many predators anyway because he tastes really awful.

"The larvae taste better than their parents, but they've discovered a way to keep from being eaten. The larvae smear themselves with poop. Seriously.

Their own poop. So if you see little piles of poop walking around on the underside of a lily leaf, you're not crazy. What you see are just larvae dressed in their poop suits. It's the price you have to pay to stay alive. But what do I know?"

"If I had to choose between walking around under a blanket of poop or dying, I think I'd rather die."

"Yes, I agree with the wild donkey. I'm slow enough as it is, but if I were covered by a layer of poop, I'd come to a complete standstill."

"Huh? Am I seeing things?"

"Yeah. How did you get here all of a sudden?"

"The hermit crab and the rose-ringed parakeet asked if I'd please come back."

"Have I missed anything?"

"Yes, mole. Stop spending all your time underground. The Gila monster is back!"

"Super cool!"

"Totally awesome!"

"Yeah, totally awesome, it's unanimous!"

"Well, you heard it, Gila monster. We all welcome you back. We're curious about your presentation, but we're still listening to the fruit fly."

"I'm almost done. The scarlet lily beetle isn't among the endangered animals, so that's good news. Not for humans, though, because for them the scarlet lily beetle is a pest. But what do we care what humans think? Let the beetles enjoy their food. That's what plants are for, right? But that's just my humble opinion.

"If a scarlet lily beetle does get attacked, he lets go of the plant and drops to the ground, where he pretends he's dead. He folds up his legs and makes sure he's lying on his back. That way the predator can't see his red wing case, only his black belly. He uses his black belly as camouflage, because it blends with the dark earth where lily plants grow. Very clever idea.

"Are you a fan of red animals, too? Then check out the fire-colored beetles. Some of them are also a beautiful red. Well, that was my presentation. Are there any questions?

"Yes!"

"Let's have it, zebra."

"Are there any black-and-white beetles?"

"Well, you have the Maybugs and the June bugs. They're brownish. But there's also the pine chafer. They come close to black-and-white, but only close."

"So I didn't forget to include them in my presentation?"

"No, because their black isn't orca or panda black, and their white isn't badger or skunk white."

"Thank goodness."

"Forgetting something is no big deal, zebra, because if you forget something, you can always go back and make up for it or correct it."

"I like to get it right the first time, fruit fly."

"Then you lucked out, because I really can't think of any black-and-white beetles. Any more questions?"

"No, but I do want to say something to you."

"Go ahead, southern cassowary."

"If you're small, like the hummingbird, you also have a right to an opinion, so you don't have to keep saying that your opinion is small or humble or mini or less valuable because you're only a fruit fly."

"Thank you very much. I'll keep that in mind."

"We all thought it was a great presentation, didn't we, animals?"

"Yes, barn owl, we thought it was tremendous!"

"Super cool!"

"Thank you, worm."

"Colossal, ha-ha-ha-ha!"

"Titanic! And as a blue whale I should know."

"Top grades for the fruit fly."

"Thank you, everyone. I'm glowing."

# 20

## "Hello,
## I'm a Gila monster
## and I'm finally
## giving my
## presentation on
## the..."

"We're sorry, Gila monster."

"Yes, we apologize."

"We all apologize. We just got scared."

"Yes, and we don't even know who scared us. Somehow it got started, and then everybody joined in."

"It was crazy. Everybody—really. Because we were afraid. We didn't do it on purpose or anything. Like the hermit crab said, everybody eats everybody else, more or less. That's sort of how life works."

"And the weird thing is that as a yellow scorpion I'm more poisonous than you are. And still I went along with it."

"Yes, same with me."

"Me, too!"

"Me, too!"

"Settle down, cobra, pufferfish, and poison dart frog. We are who we are, and everybody knows that all of you are much more poisonous. I think the Gila monster gets it. So he can go ahead and start talking without being nervous."

"Thank you, barn owl. In that case I'm going to start my presentation on

## THE BLUE SEA DRAGON."

"Isn't that one of those made-up mythical creatures like the unicorn?"

"No, starfish, the blue sea dragon really exists."

"Cool!"

"Yes, fox, he's really cool. Now if you don't mind, I'm going to start.

"The blue sea dragon is a slug. A sea slug without a shell. He doesn't breathe fire, but he does spit poison. He doesn't make the poison himself, though, like all the other poisonous animals do. The poison of the blue sea dragon is stolen. Stolen from one of the most feared animals in the sea."

"This presentation is already *amazing*."

"Thank you, fox. The blue sea dragon is an animal as big as, uh . . . the beak of the barn owl. And his name says it all: He's bright blue. But only his belly. His back is silver white. He can't swim very well, so he floats on the surface of the ocean. He lives in all the seas on earth that aren't too cold.

"Because the sea water looks blue from the sky, the blue sea dragon swims on his back, with his blue belly facing upward and acting as camouflage. And his silver white back doesn't stand out if you're looking up from the bottom of the sea. You might say, why isn't it the other way around? Why does the blue sea dragon swim upside down to camouflage himself? Why didn't they make his back blue and his belly silver white? Well, why not? I have no idea."

"There's something I've been wondering about, too."

"What's that, wild donkey?"

"Why megabats and other bats hang upside down, like blue sea dragons."

"Some animals just do their thing upside down, I guess. Nature is really peculiar, wild donkey. But let me continue.

"The blue sea dragon has a little balloon in his belly that's filled with gas, and that's how he's able to float on the surface of the water.

"Attached to his body are six, uh . . . they aren't legs or fins or feathers. They're more like little fans. I don't know what else to call them. All I can say is, this animal is totally different from any other animal, so you just have to believe me.

"The blue sea dragon likes jellyfish, and his favorite jellyfish is the deadly Portuguese man o' war. That animal is a whole nother story. The Portuguese man o' war is an animal that's put together from several different animals. Each of the animals forms a different part. Really strange. He's super poisonous, and some of his tentacles are as long as a whale. He uses the tentacles to catch fish, first by harpooning them. Then he paralyzes the fish with the poison in the harpoons."

"Hey, that's funny."

"What's funny, leaf insect?"

"Well, remember when I told you during my presentation that the sea anemone also has harpoons?"

"Oh, yeah. These are the same sort of harpoons, leaf insect."

"Okay, animals. Focus, please."

"Thank you, barn owl. Now I'm going to tell you how the blue sea dragon operates. It's super technical. So he really likes the Portuguese man o' war, which is much bigger than he is. Even so, the blue sea dragon attacks that giant jellyfish. The blue sea dragon is one of the few animals that isn't hurt by the poison of the Portuguese man o' war.

"He attaches himself to his victim with his mouth. Inside his mouth is a radula. That's a fancy name for a tongue with tiny teeth. So the blue sea dragon has a tongue that works like a scraper. His whole mouth is full of these scrapers, which he uses to gobble up the entire Portuguese man o' war, bit by bit. Harpoons and all."

"Whoo-hoo!"

"Wait a minute, fox. I'm not even finished.

"Now something really unusual happens in the blue sea dragon's body. In his stomach he digests the little harpoons, along with the rest of the jelly-fish. But he lets the biggest harpoons flow into the six fans on either side of his body. Think of the six fans as warehouses for the harpoons. Those storage areas make the blue sea dragon more poisonous than ever. Because the more bits of jellyfish he eats, the more poison gets stored in his fans. How cool is that?"

"Awesome!"

"Exactly, fox, super awesome.

"Now maybe you think that the blue sea dragon is the most dangerous animal in the sea, but actually he's not so bad. He is dangerous, no question about it, but he uses his poison to defend himself, just like me. So if you give him a hard time, you'll be in big trouble, but if you just admire him from a distance, he'll leave you alone.

"So, that's it for today. I want to thank everyone for paying attention. This was my presentation on the blue sea dragon. Questions, anybody?"

"Yes!"

"Let's have it, rabbit."

"Well, we all want to learn something about the children of the blue sea dragon."

"Speak for yourself, rabbit. I couldn't care less."

"Well, when I say 'we,' I don't mean you, howler monkey. I mean 'us': all the rabbits."

"That's a good question, rabbit. What you first need to know is that the blue sea dragon is both male and female."

"Awesome!"

"Yeah, friggin' awesome."

"Animals, animals. Watch your language."

"A blue sea dragon has eggs, like all females. But the blue sea dragon also has a penis."

"Yuck!"

"No, hummingbird, there's nothing disgusting or weird about that. And it doesn't mean they produce young by mating with themselves. For that they need a partner."

"We earthworms do the same thing. We sort of give children to each other. Earthworms have both eggs and sperm in their bodies. If we meet up with another earthworm, we exchange sperm with each other to fertilize our own eggs. And then we lay the eggs in a safe place underground."

"But wait a minute. I'm a leaf insect, and I *can* produce offspring on my own."

"You mean all by yourself?"

"Yes, fox, all by myself. I don't need a male."

"Wow! How cool is that?"

"Well, we rabbits think it's much more fun doing it together."

"That's what most animals think, rabbit. Let me finish my answer to your question. Blue sea dragons lay about twenty eggs on whatever is floating in the water: a piece of wood or the remains of a jellyfish. A bit of a Portuguese man o' war, for instance. That way the young have something to eat as soon as they hatch. Handy, right? Any more questions?"

"You really know a lot, Gila monster. I have one more question."

"Go ahead, barn owl."

"Are blue sea dragons still poisonous when they're dead? And if they can't swim very well, how do they make their way to a Portuguese man o' war?

And does the blue sea dragon live all alone in the sea, or do they float around in groups?"

"Yes, barn owl. When they're dead and they wash up on shore, they're still poisonous and their sting still hurts.

"Second bit: they let the wind and the waves push them along. But if they get close to a jellyfish, they can use their fans to paddle up to it. So they can swim, but only short distances.

"And then part three of your question: they live alone, but sometimes they do things together. They feed together on the same prey, for example. And while they're at it, they often take the opportunity to exchange sperm with each other.

"A single one of these animals is called a blue sea dragon. But if they're all lumped together, they're called a blue fleet.

"So that's it. I've told you everything I know. This was my presentation. Thank you for listening. I don't feel excluded anymore."

"A round of applause for the Gila monster!"

"That was really cool!"

"Super cool!"

"Love you, Gila monster."

"Yeah, big heart for the Gila monster."

"Thank you. I'm glad I came back. A round of applause for the rose-ringed parakeet and the hermit crab, who encouraged me. And thank you, barn owl, for keeping everything focused."

"I have just one more question."

"Go ahead, worm."

"Are we going to give more presentations next year too, because I thought this was really great."

"Yes. Then I can tell you a little more about the regal blue tang."

"Maybe we should vote on it."

"Yeah. Let's have presentations by other animals—besides giving the hermit crab a second chance."

"Good idea, giraffe."

"Yes, good idea!"

"Super good!"

"Who goes first?"

"Me!"

"Who?"

"Me!"

"Terrific, maned wolf. We're already looking forward to it."

"Till next year, everybody! But let's agree on one thing."

"What's that, barn owl?"

"That we're not going to keep interrupting each and every presentation."

"But that's impossible, barn owl."

"Yes, impossible."

"YEAH, BARN OWL. IM-FRIGGIN'-POSSIBLE!"

# ONE LAST THING...

"Animals, aren't we missing something?"

"We're not going to thank anyone, are we, barn owl?"

"No. The only ones we have to thank are ourselves. But shouldn't we do something to make all these presentations a bit more organized?"

"How do we do that?"

"Well, by creating an index, for example."

"What's that?"

"An index is a list of names that comes at the end of a book. Like which animal is mentioned on what page. Or which animal says something in what chapter."

"Sounds like a good idea. I really like it when things are organized."

"So maybe this is a job for you, midwife toad?"

"Why not me?"

"Because the only animal on your list would be yourself, snow leopard! That's why."

"You should talk, fox!"

"You can count me out on helping. There are already twenty sharks lined up at my door."

"I only talk about black-and-white animals, so this is not for me."

"I'm too busy with my hummingbird collection."

"I think I might be too small to work on a list like this."

"No one is ever too small for anything, fruit fly, but it is a big job."

"I'd like to be involved, too, barn owl."

"That's great, worm. You two want to work together on this? Is everybody happy with the worm and the midwife toad making an index?"

"Yes!"

"Me, too!"

"Fine by me."

"Super fine. I'm glad they want to do this."

"Yeah, super duper fine."

"Very good. Then we can end this book in an organized fashion."

"Just one more question, barn owl."

"What is it, worm?"

"Should the animals who've said something on this page be included in the index? Like the 'super duper fine' from the fox, for example?"

"No, worm, you can ignore that, because the fox is probably going to be mentioned more than anyone else in the index anyway."

"You should talk, barn owl."

"Animals, animals. There are talkers and there are listeners. All the white parts on these pages are the listeners. The black parts are the talkers. One can't do without the other, you might say. No black without white, and no white without black."

"Well said, barn owl. Words after my own heart."

"Thank you, zebra."

"We think it's all great!"

"Yeah, super great."

"Okay, fox, let's hear it. Ha-ha-ha-ha!"

## "SUPER DUPER GREAT!"

"Ha-ha-ha-ha-ha-ha-ha-ha-ha-ha-ha-ha!"

# INDEX*

(made by the earthworm and the midwife toad)

"So if I understand this correctly, we have to make a list of all the animals mentioned and put them in alphabetical order?"

"Yup, that's the idea, worm."

"But should I list myself under the 'e' for earthworm or the 'w' for worm?"

"That's a good question. I have the same problem. Am I a toad in the index, or a midwife toad?"

"And the rhinoceros is a family with five species. So do we list the white and the black rhinoceros under 'r,' or under 'w' and 'b'?"

"And there are different species of zebras, too."

"How about the three hundred species of hummingbirds? We'd have to fill the whole index with

the hummingbird alphabet just to make the southern cassowary happy! From the Amazilia hummingbird to the white-bearded helmetcrest to the—"

"There are also different species of fireflies,
swans, woodpeckers, cleaner fish . . ."

"You know what, midwife toad? I don't think we
should make such a big deal out of this."

"But it has to be accurate, worm."

"That's true. I have an idea."

"Let's hear it."

"If we call the animals by the same name that was
used to identify them in their presentations, we're
all set, right?"

"So you mean: the white rhinoceros and the wild
donkey go under 'w'? And the zebra just goes under
'z' because in the presentations there's no mention
of the Grévy's zebra, the plains zebra, or the mountain zebra?"

"Exactly. So you go under 'm.' Along with the mole and the megabat."

"And you go under the 'e'?"

"Yes. Even though I'm also called 'worm,' I'd rather be listed under the 'e' for earthworm."

"And then the very last question: what do we do about the hummingbirds?"

"We'll list them all under the 'h' of the hummingbird family. Sorry, southern cassowary."

"Okay, that's it, worm. We can get started."

"Let's get after it, midwife toad."

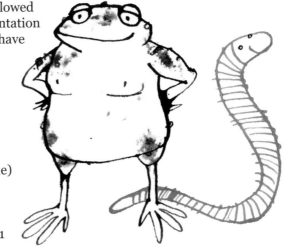

* Each animal's name is followed by the number of the presentation they give, or in which they have something to say.

# A

Adélie penguin 5
alligator 16
anaconda ♥ 10, 17
anemone (see sea anemone)
ant 14
anteater 16
Asian badger 5
Atlantic spotted dolphin 11

"This is going well, worm."

"Yes, especially that cross-reference for the anemone. Let's do that for the worm, too."

"Good idea."

"Super good. Ha-ha-ha!"

# B

badger 5, 19
barn cat 14
barn owl 8, 9, 10, 11, 12, 13, 14, 15, 17, 18, 19, 20
barn swallow 14

barnacle goose 9
bats (family) 8, 13, 18, 20
Batman hoverfly 11
bear 12, 14
bitterling 12
bittern 3
black-and-white ruffed lemur 5

blackbird 2, 3, 8
black mamba 17
black rhinoceros 16
blue sea dragon 20
blue whale 19
boa constrictor 10
brant goose 9
buffalo 14, 17
butterfly 5, 1
buzzard 3

## C

caiman 10
California kingsnake 5
camel 10
capybara 10
cat 14
chiffchaff 3
cleaner fish 1, 18
cobra 17, 20
colobus monkey 5
common redpoll 3
common ringed plover 11
cow 14
coyote 17
crocodile 18
crow 2, 8

## D

daddy long-legs 8
death's-head hawkmoth 13, 19
death's-head monkey (see squirrel
   monkey)

deer 6, 10, 18
dwarf cassowary 11

## E

earthworm 8, 10, 15, 19, 20
edible dormouse 10
Egyptian goose 9
elephant 6, 12
ermine 5
European badger 5
European green woodpecker 8
European hoverfly 11

## F

false cleaner fish 1
fire-colored beetle 19
firefly 7
flamingo 16
flying fox 18
fox 1, 9, 10, 13, 14, 15, 17, 18, 19, 20
fruit fly 18, 19

## G

gerbil 17
Gila monster 17, 18, 19, 20
giraffe 18, 20
golden eagle 17
Golfodulcean poison frog 11
goose 3, 9, 14
graylag goose 28, 73
great spotted woodpecker 8
great white shark 12

nightjar 13
northern cassowary 11
Norwegian Forest cat 14

# O

octopus 1
okapi 8
orangutan 18
orca 5, 19
osprey 5
ostrich 3

# P

panda 5, 19
parasite 1
pelican 16
penguin 8
perch 10
pied butterfly bat 5
pied hoverfly 11
pine chafer 19
pink-footed goose 9
piranha 10, 12
plankton 17
poison dart frog 20
Portuguese man o' war 20
possum 4
pufferfish 20
puma 13

# Q

quail 17

# R

rabbit 4, 14, 20
rat 14
rattlesnake 17
raven 3
regal blue tang 7, 20
reindeer 15
rhinoceros (family) 6, 18
robin 3
rose-ringed parakeet 2, 3, 18, 19, 20

# S

Savi's warbler 3
scarlet lily beetle 19
sea anemone 15
seagull 14, 17
sea slug 15, 20
shark 1, 12, 14, 18
sheep 10
shoebill 16
shrimp 15, 17
skunk 5, 19
sloth 18
snow goose 9
snow leopard 6, 17, 18, 20
songbirds 2, 3
song thrush 3
southern cassowary 11, 12, 19
sparrow 3, 13
spider 14
spoonbill 16
spotted hyena 11
spotted python 11
squirrel monkey 13

starfish 12, 20
starling 8
stork 5, 16
Sumatran rhinoceros 16
swan 3
sword-billed hummingbird 11, 12

## T

tang (see regal blue tang)
Tasmanian devil 14
tawny owl 3
tick 18
tiger 12, 18
tortoise 8, 10, 17

## U

unicorn 12

## V

vole 9

## W

walking stick 15
wallaby 14

water flea 16
whale 12, 20
whinchat 3
whip-poor-will 3
white-beaked dolphin 11
white rhinoceros 16
wild boar 8
wild cat 14
wild donkey 16, 17, 18,
    19, 20
wild duck 18
wild fox (see fox)
wild horse 18
wolf 6, 12, 17
wolverine 14
woodpeckers (family) 3
worm (see earthworm)
wren 3

## Y

yellow scorpion 17, 20

## Z

zebra 5, 16, 18, 19
zebra long-winged
    butterfly 5

"A round of applause for the worm and the midwife
toad!"

"May I say something, please?"

"Go right ahead, worm."

"Next year can we have some animals that start
with X?"

"Good idea, worm."

"Yeah, super good idea!"

**Bibi Dumon Tak** writes nonfiction, or as she calls it: the truth in stories. Most of those stories are about animals. And all those stories are true. They are about cows that have escaped from slaughter; about animals that help people in times of war; about birds, arctic animals, uncuddly animals, cloven-hoofed animals, city animals. She has no preferences. As long as it can crawl, fly, swim or run; as long as it has fur, scales, spines or feathers. As long as they aren't people.

Dumon Tak has won the Gouden Griffel, the highest honor for children's books in the Netherlands, as well as the Theo Thijssen Prize, the highest honor for authors. Two books of hers, *Soldier Bear* and *Mikis and the Donkey*, have won the Mildred L. Batchelder Award.

**Annemarie van Haeringen** is a leading Dutch illustrator and author. She has illustrated numerous children's books and worked on films and children's magazines. She has won the Gouden Penseel—the highest honor for children's illustration in the Netherlands—three times, and her books have been published in more than twenty-five languages.

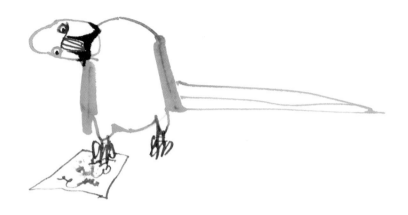

**Nancy Forest-Flier** is an American-born translator and editor living and working in the Netherlands. She has translated several adult and children's novels from Dutch to English as well as books of historical nonfiction. She has also translated for numerous Dutch museums and institutes including the Anne Frank House. She has six children and ten grandchildren.

# SOME NOTES ON THIS BOOK'S PRODUCTION

The art for the jacket, case, and interiors was created by Annemarie van Haeringen using a variety of techniques to make them look as good as possible, usually with a basis of pen, inks, and Ecoline and watercolor paints. The snow leopard was done as a large drawing on colored paper, with white watercolor paint and India ink for the spots; colored pencil was used for the legs of the Adelie penguin; the blackbird was torn from black paper; a comb was used for the unicorn's mane; and so on. The text was set by Westchester Publishing Services, in Danbury, CT, in Georgia a typeface created in 1993 for Microsoft by British designer Matthew Carter. Inspired by 19th century Scotch Romans designs, the name of this serif refers to a tabloid headline, "Alien heads found in Georgia." The display was set in Wilbert, a typeface created by Petra Santaharju that includes slab serif and sans serif influences as well as accents and special letters from many different languages. The book was printed on FSC™-certified 120gsm Golden Sun woodfree paper and bound in China.

Production supervised by Freesia Blizard
Book designed by Ally Thatcher
Assistant Managing Editor: Danielle Maldonado
Editor: Nick Thomas

LEVINE QUERIDO

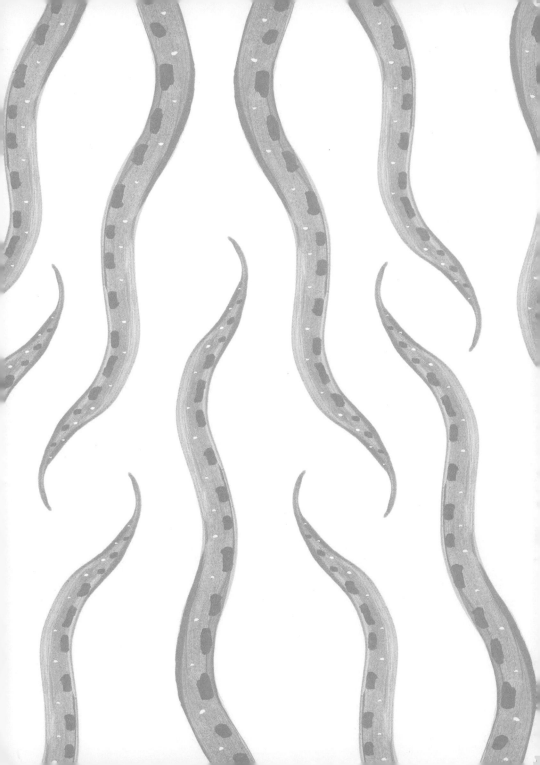